A LINE IN THE SAND

Stories of Boundaries in Marriage

A catalogue record for this book is available from the National Library of Nigeria.

ISBN: 978-978-987-869-7

Published in Nigeria by WORITAL GLOBAL, 2021
13a Baptist Church Street, Gbagada Phase 2, Lagos, Nigeria.
WORITAL (hello@worital.com)
+2348114027024

Cover Design, Layout, Printed and Bound by:
WORITAL (hello@worital.com)

To my parents, Efua & Seiyifa Koroye,
For the honor, respect and love you share.
Thank you for your practical example of **boundaries**,
Before I ever knew of the concept.

PRAISE FOR "A LINE IN THE SAND"

"Bralade is an amazing storyteller & exceptional communicator. She demonstrates this mastery in her debut book as she unveils time-less secrets that have helped families become dynasties through enduring & lasting relationships. We need more books like this to shed light on topics that are pivotal in supporting healthy marriages and family values, for transgenerational impact. The fact that we get to read these stories through a rich cultural lens makes it all the more refreshing and relatable."

- **FELA DUROTOYE,** *Business Consultant, Leadership Expert, and Motivational Speaker.*

"The author of this collection of short stories started writing when she was a child. She was only 10 when she handed her father (me!) an exercise book filled with stories she had written. With this collection, I believe that Bralade has launched herself as a writer with a promising future. The stories are all direct in their presentation of action and emotion, and in their portrayal of character, so that at the end of each story we come away with a sense of a complete action. A brilliant debut!"

- **SEIYIFA KOROYE,** *Literary Critic.*

Bralade has undressed stigmas, fears, questions, love, life, and wisdom. Despite the many wonders in "A Line in the Sand", I believe the biggest gift might be the healing that truth will bring to you. You would feel seen, understood, and loved. You might find yourself forgiving yourself... this is an un-put-down-able type of art; scripted delicately with brilliance, suspense, soul-deep writing, and love.

I challenge you to keep an open mind, and start from the Author's Notes, because you will find gems for your journey. Like an elder, the wisdom is not forced on you, yet it will stream into your heart quietly. I loved reading "A Line in the Sand" from start to finish, first because I love heart-warming fiction, but also because I love Bralade who's become a dearly beloved sister and friend to me.

I hope millions of my brothers and sisters all over the planet lay their hands on this book as well, because it teaches all of us how precious our humanity is, as well as the responsibility we have to nurture our lives with intentional love, deliberate kindness and personal agency.

- DEBOLA DEJI-KURUNMI, *Author, Coach and Public PolicyAdvisor*

There is a delicious paradox in each beautifully crafted story in 'A Line in the Sand'. The themes, the characters, the complex issues it deals with are all so achingly familiar and yet the unfolding of each plot startles us! Bralade has managed to gently and artfully take us on a journey of exploration of the bogeymen that leaves us acting or making choices contrary to our own interests in relationships- fear, culture, masculinity, sisterhood, religion, patriarchy. We have been gifted in this brilliant collection, not just a truly satisfying literary experience, but also an open door to start new conversations.

- PROF. ENGOBO EMESEH, *University of Bradford.*

Stories project important conversations. These mirror events and problems of financial strain, delayed conception, verbal abuse, in-law theatrics, religious manipulation, and relationship stress. While unveiling each plot and conclusion, she delivers one consistent message: Boundaries Matter! This important message around understanding our sanity limits, and respectfully communicating our deal breakers is as necessary as it is now urgent.

- **EDEN A. ONWUKA,** *Author, Relationship and Mindset Coach.*

"Because I saw myself and several people I know in the pages of Line in the Sand, I kept on reading until the very end. Bralade has written fourteen beautiful stories in a style that is uniquely hers... Lovers of lucid writing, courageous people will love what she has done."

- **MICHAEL AFENFIA,** *Author, The Mechanics of Yenagoa*

It would have been okay for Bralade to just teach the incredible lessons on boundaries she shares here, but she was gracious enough, awesome enough to wrap it all in delicious story telling that is every readers dream.

- **LAJU IREN,** *Bestselling Author, Book writing Coach & Film maker*

The stories paint a vivid picture of possibilities and problems in marriages. Boundaries are critical for a successful thriving relationship and Bralade's stories highlight this fact. This book is a great read with a transformational message.

- **EKENE ONU,** *Leadership Consultant & Executive Coach.*

In her first book, A Line In The Sand, Bralade skillfully narrates testimonies of love in a way that rekindles our belief in destiny and the ability of people to find each other no matter where, when or how.

- **EBI AKPETI,** *Author, The Perfect Church.*

Bralade is an amazing woman with a strong drive and a life changing passion. Her words and perspective are truly unparalleled. If you have ever been at a crossroads in your relationship and you're looking to be understood you picked up the right book!

- DR NICOLYA WILLIAMS, *Bestselling Author & Master Life Coach.*

Rising from the ashes of servitude as a phoenix. Reinventing oneself. Envisioning and implementing limits. These are tenets that Bralade lives by. As a woman of many talents, teaching and inspiring others to achieve their very own enlightenment is a passion of hers. With a superb grasp on the topic of boundaries, she espouses wisdom which she abides by in her burgeoning career and life. As a biased observer and cheerleader, this collection of well woven stories shows only a fraction of her nigh infinite talent, drive, and oratorical skill.

- OBIOHA EMENANJO, *Spouse and Faithful Cheerleader.*

In this book, Bralade uses compelling stories to drive home a subject that we hardly hear enough of - Boundaries! Be warned, it is a can't-drop-it-till-you're-done kinda book!

- OMONIKORO, *Event/Radio Host.*
Convener, the Little Genius Championship.

Thank you, Bralade for this priceless gift to the world and for showing us that we are not alone, no matter the demons we are fighting. This is a movement! A campaign! A much-needed conversation.

- IJEAWELE CHIMAMAKA OGBONNA, *Founder, Ikoro-Igboamaka (Society, Culture & Language Platform)*

This book is a campaign for more self-worth; it is a compass in identifying broken boundaries and a reminder to set the limit before adversity and wrong influences erodes one's core. Thank you for bringing this gift to our world.

- SHOLA AMARAIBI, *Poet & Author.*

AUTHOR'S NOTE

Hello,

I am Bralade and it's lovely to meet you. Let me share with you: my thoughts on boundaries, the background of this book and what I trust you will glean from it.

I am convinced, beyond a shadow of doubt, that you are worthy. That you are more than enough. That you are to be respected as a human yet divine entity. Firmly rooted in my faith is the knowledge that the uniqueness of God is breathed into every woman and man. It is this belief that moves me to appreciate the principles and psychology of boundaries.

I first encountered the phrase in a series of books and teachings by Christian psychologists, Drs Henry Cloud and John Townsend. The concept of Boundaries as the line strengthening two people, rather than separating them was fascinating to me. How a person can own the responsibility to define themselves is gold to any individual seeking self-actualization and developing healthy relationships. It all buttressed my faith in the personal power of the individual as the ultimate change agent of their lives.

As a chemical engineer, I know a bit about chemical reactions. You see, some reactions require a reagent or reactant to cause a change while polymerization reactions need no other substance. Rather, they cause a super-long chain of the same molecules to be formed, in the presence of energy. While inherently the same substance, the bonds cause a completely new material to be formed: strong and solid: just as how the gas ethylene becomes the solid, polyethylene.

Now, breathe. I said all that sciencey stuff to explain this: the most powerful change can occur right within you and not necessarily, without. If you realize your personal power and own your identity by defining and setting healthy boundaries, you would be solid, stable and strong as an individual. Capable of saying and meaning your NO. Owning and wholeheartedly saying your YES. **Refusing a life of people pleasing because at your core is a compass able to withstand external influence.** You will be able to stay true to your values consistently across relationships.

Against this backdrop, I inadvertently set out on a crusade, to get people to become more accountable for their desired transformations. I have been sharing, teaching and coaching this message for almost a decade. On the heels of the tenth anniversary of marriage to a truly interesting and phenomenal young man, Obioha, I decided to write a book on marriage with the theme of boundaries.

However, I realized that no two relationships or marriages are the same and that each person's solution or path lies in their hands. Or more accurately, the knowledge they possess and act upon. I also believed that the principles were already taught by the experts and there was no need to repeat them. Sure, it would make me seem knowledgeable but if you could not see yourself or your story in it, I doubted it would be of much use to you.

And that's how this book was born. I believe you will see yourself, your family or your friend in at least one of these fourteen couples, who reach defining moments in their relationships where they had to draw the proverbial Line in the Sand.

When I took my pen to write on paper (interesting fact: no Word processor or computer screen interfaced with my first draft), these characters started telling me their stories, I could feel their discontent and they guided me through the transformation they inevitably faced. I meandered their quagmires with them and explored possibilities. I saw through assumed villains and self-proclaimed victims. I saw that most wanted great marriages but struggled to find out how.

I bring you that raw honesty and human experience in these stories. You will laugh, cry, curse and shout as you sit on the stands and watch them navigate the disruption that came to their lives. You may even blame some or excuse others. In a space full of "let me tell you what to do" books, I know you will learn something that only you can glean. I trust you. I trust your ability. That you can apply your learnings from this book to your unique context.

I do hope that through their stories, you find the vulnerability to tell your story and the courage to draw your own line in the sand. As you honor your boundaries, the road may seem bleak at first, as you will see in the stories, but I promise you, your future would thank you for it.

If boundaries were only selfish and self-aggrandizing, they would not be worth it. Rather, boundaries are the basis on which you are free to love, be loved and live the life of impact you truly want, here on earth.

I have enjoyed a largely healthy marriage with my husband, Obi but we have not been without our share of trials and adversity. We found that boundaries were needed there too because couples with special needs children experience a higher rate of trouble or breakup. In fact, the title story, A Line in The Sand is a memoir of sorts, telling our story.

True culture shaping comes from telling stories and rich learning is entrenched by sharing our experiences, so I leave you with this final word which I have paraphrased "Tell your children (friends) about it, And let your children (friends) tell their children (friends), And their children (friends) the next generation." (Joel 1:3). For the best experience, get some friends and family to read this book with.

I have included some additional resources with this book. In the appendix, you will find an action guide on how to set boundaries in marriage, so you have the tools to apply these skills. Followed by a glossary section for ease of word reference.

I would love to hear your thoughts and be a part of your boundaries conversation. Kindly send me an email, leave a review, invite me to your book club, get more resources on my website at www.bralade.com. And finally, keep telling your stories because they matter.

CONTENTS

EVERY WOMAN'S DREAM MAN

The day I left was the day he called his mother a witch and hung up on her. His handsome face, the color of mahogany, was set in a determined mask. I could see the sods of the spittle at the corner of his mouth, from when he was cursing at his mother. I could faintly hear her feebly trying to defend and explain something on the other side of the call.

This time I did not cry. This time I did not feel the chills from the shock of disgust and astonishment I had felt the first time

I experienced his outburst. This time, I just felt the weariness of someone who had been hanging on to a ledge for hours.

It felt like the scales were falling off, as if someone pulled back the curtains on the starkness of truth. In the same way you cannot unsee a naked person who was inadvertently exposed; I knew there was no going back on the reality of Timiebi's character. I did not even feel the weight of my resolve. It was as if the decision had been made for me. I realized the numbness I felt was in the inevitability of what had to happen.

I slowly got up and started walking towards the door. He was still mumbling, "I will not have anyone talk to me anyhow... when I make a decision, it is final!" He continued pacing, "Dem never born the person wey go try me, rubbish! Nonsense! I don't care who you are, I will tell you my mind, and insult your generation very well." He was fuming and working himself up even more.

I was quietly picking up my book where I had left it. It was the dog-eared wedding planning journal with the details of the event I have been planning for almost seven months. It felt like seven years ago, now that I think about it. It was hard to remember the time before then, or the gorgeous dude that had asked me to marry him while on one knee, with a saxophonist serenading us. Funny now that I think about it, he didn't wait for my response, before he slipped the ring on and my gleeful yes was lost in the cheers of friends and family he had gathered at the Lagoon Club.

My mind flashed back to the proposal. We had been in a fight the night before, so I was not expecting it. It was a huge argument where he had called me the B-Word and 'ungrateful'. I did not think we were going to get back together again. I knew it was seriously wrong. So when our mutual friend who incidentally introduced us told me to pick her up at the social club where our families have been members since we were little kids, I had to muster the strength to leave the house.

I had stood up, wiped my tears, and driven the fifteen minutes to the club, thinking how to break the news to Layefa, who apparently thought we were the perfect couple, not necessarily because we were compatible, but because we were the perfectly sculpted power-couple; both doctors, he a consultant of ophthalmology while I, a third year pediatrics resident at LUTH.

Timiebi and I are both from the same Bayelsa State, and though our parents did not know each other, when we were introduced, he was familiar. In that vain way that a member of your social class appears like a cultural fit. We shared medicine and experiences from private universities. We shared tales of annual vacations abroad. And we never lacked what to talk about, or rather, he never run out of topics to discuss. And I loved listening, so it was not a hard thing to do. I was jolted back to reality as the huge stonework sign of Lagos Lagoon Club loomed on my path. I indicated, turned off the road and made it safely to the car lot where Layefa had directed me to come towards. A quick glance around and I realized that her classy teal Kia Soul was nowhere around. A bit miffed, I picked up the phone to call her. She should have let me know she had made other plans, today was not the day!

She picked up on second ring. "Alaere, where are you now?"
I responded, exasperated, "where else, of course, where you said you would be."
She said, "Don't be angry now... I'm inside."
"So come out now." I replied, my impatience betrayed by my tone.

"No, you come inside. There's something I want you to see. I hope you dressed nicely as I told you?" She asked, ignoring my impatience. I could swear she was wearing that annoying grin now.

"What room are you in?" I heard the click as she had cut the call. I groaned. I was not in the mood for games, but I extracted the lip gloss from the glove compartment of my 2018 Toyota RAV4, cursing under my breath. Thankfully, I had a spare wig in my car that I pulled on and gave a quick pat before I stepped out.

At the lobby, someone asked, “Are you Alaere?”
“Yes” I replied gratefully, because I did not know which of the six wings to start looking from, as I followed him.

“SURPRISE!!!” Everyone shouted as I walked in the room, and only my frozen shocked state kept my feet planted at a spot. I started spotting the familiar faces in the crowd. There was my chief resident and Aunty Preye, my brother and my cousins, our parents. I was still bewildered and wondering whether my birthday - which was another two months away - was worth all this, when Timiebi came through the small crowd. He walked through a makeshift rose-petaled aisle and fell on one knee in the path of the flowers that stopped right in front of me.

As I figured out what was happening, my confusion doubled. He approached me slowly, his eyes fixed on mine as He slowly approached and said, “Alaere, my beautiful girl. I knew from the first day I met you that you would be my wife. I love you so much, and I want you to be mine for always, marry me.”

My fairy tale was happening in the moment. And I was swept up in the fulfilment of the dream I had nursed since my secondary school days of Mills & Boons; looking around the room and seeing the approving faces and celebratory cheers only affirmed my decision, or the decision that was made for me because he was already slipping the ring on as I said, "Yes!"

Looking back now, there was no question to respond to, just another one of his commands.

After the uber romantic proposal, and the cocktail that followed at a club with family and friends. I had playfully asked him, "Is it not you that insulted me yesterday now acting like a knight in shining armour?" Immediately I said it, the regret came in droves.

He went from his boyish grin to eyes narrowing and flashing in anger, "Are you seriously bringing that up? Just be grateful that I overlooked your little tantrum," He continued, "you are about to be a married woman now, you better grow up and start acting like one don't EVER walk out on me again. Next time I won't forgive as easily." he ended with a warning.

My Aunty Preye was coming close, so I managed an apologetic smile as I linked my hands with his, trying to keep up appearances. I also remember his Uncle Oweila as well, with his robust laughter saying

"It's only a good girl like you that can marry Timiebi's hot head o." And everyone had laughed approvingly like I was a special angel breed from heaven, devoid of hurt or anger, and suitably long suffering to be called a wife.

The whirlwind of wedding planning had started with a flurry of activities. Layefa had convened our friends in a WhatsApp group, and soon, *asoebi* outfit choices were being evaluated. And there was talk of specially choreographed dance that I made clear was not a desire of mine and I was not a willing party to.

"You dey fear?" Erica had smirked. "Don't worry, we will give you the easy steps. This one that you cannot even do simple *owigiri,*" she stated. "You think we want you to embarrass us?"

I burst out laughing. Only in the Nigerian party scene do guests get to think that an event bears a direct representation of them. They become almost like ambassadors of events they attend; proudly displaying expensive souvenirs and speaking about the performing musicians like they paid for them. On the other hand, if it were flop, they would almost deny that they went there. This was the proverbial good child who had many parents versus the failure one who nobody wanted.

Such was my wedding plan progress when the chink started turning to fault-sized cracks in the armour.

The first family feud happened at the introduction. This is an event where the close family of the groom came to formally be introduced to the bride's family, and state their intention of marriage; an intimate event which holds at the home of the bride's parents, and after all pleasantries a list for the bride price items would be received by the groom's family; that would usually be in difference as the obliging party that came to seek the proverbial golden flower.

It started with my dad announcing that the customary traditional wedding would hold in our hometown of Sagbama. He had declared amidst the festivities, and upon receiving cases of beverage gifts, "All roads lead to Sagbama for the wedding of the year!"

My parents were so proud of the house, which had been recently renovated. It had a humongous living room, which seemed to me like a quarter of a soccer field. He would often justify the size of it, saying, "My daughters will marry from this house now. Where would the guests sit?" You would think he was marrying them out every single month, with the effort he put into building and furnishing it.

As family and guests laughed, Timiebi blurted, "But that is almost 1000 kilometers away. I would prefer to do it here."

The spokesman from his family quickly leapt off looking abashed and tried to smooth things out. "Well, my in-law, when we get to that bridge, we will cross it."

He said with forced humor, while he turned to look at the groom sternly; beseeching and willing him to acquiesce, or at the worst, stay quiet.

But no, Timiebi did not get the memo. I could see my dad had a little tic at the side of his mouth, struggling to keep calm from the unusual show of disrespect and challenge. He managed a laugh and said, "Children of nowadays do not like the village."

Timiebi had discourteously retorted, "This has nothing to do with that. We are just being logical and practical. There is no reason to drive all the way there when everyone we know is already here. It's ridiculous."

At that point, voices raised in an uproar. It was uncharacteristic for a prospective groom to be so forthright to speak directly to the father of the intended bride. The introduction is a nuanced ceremony, guided by third party spokespeople where the groom rarely spoke except spoken to. Such was the delicateness of the event. My father's spokesman had summarily ordered him to be quiet, exchanging a few words with him while his own family struggled to get him out of the room.

I heard this story largely third-hand, from my room where I was all spruced up and waiting to be summoned to greet my soon-to-be in- laws at the end of the formalities. But when I heard the uproar, my heart sank. And I knew beyond a shadow of doubt that it was a Timiebi blow-up.

After the event, that episode raised so many questions in the family that I subsequently tried to make lame excuses for him,

'He is just blunt like that.'
'He says what he is thinking.'
'You know he went to school abroad. That's how they speak over there.'
'Mummy, please help me beg Daddy...'
'Daddy, don't you want me to marry?'

A few days later, a special emissary was sent from Timiebi's family, Uncle Oweila. He came to formally apologize to my dad, who at this point had gone from seething to concerned.

"My daughter, are you sure you want to marry this one?" he asked, looking straight at me. I quickly said, "Yes, Yes, daddy. He is very sorry."
"If he is sorry, why is he not here to apologize?" My father had asked unconvincingly.

"Maybe they told him not to come", I lied, just happy that my perfect wedding plans were back in motion. I know he accepted to smooth things over because of his daughter's happiness, or so he thought.

When I called Timiebi to tell him the good news, he just said gruffly, "I said what I said. And I stand by it. Just because he is your father does not give him the right to dictate to me."

My attempts to explain why going to my hometown meant so much to my dad fell on deaf ears. And he summarily changed the topic with an "I don't want to talk about that anymore. If you want to keep talking, then get off my phone!"

"Haba, Timiebi, has it gotten to that?" I managed.

He doubled down with "I have told you, I will not be disrespected in my own marriage. You better choose whose side you are on: your father's or mine, because I don't tolerate disloyalty."

Even the mention of him calling my dad to say thank you for the venue concession to Lagos set him off so much but as always, I put yet another pretty bow on it and left it alone as just the usual character flaw.

Timiebi had always been difficult with everybody, and I thought very wrongly, that I was the anointed person to make up for the not-so-desirable attitudes and behavior. After all, he was faithful, I reasoned, super smart with a good career and future, even though he had some disciplinary issues at his workplace, he was a professing Christian who attended church regularly, so what more did I want?

It all came to me as I heard him cuss out his mother on the phone. I wanted to be with someone I did not have to walk on eggshells around. I wanted to be with someone who respected me as much as he claimed to love me. I wanted to be around an emotionally stable person whose life was not punctuated by outbursts. Someone, who was measured, even- keeled and reasonable, who cared about the relationships in my life, and heck, his own life too.

The reality dawned that day like cold water running from my head to my toes. I knew I had to cancel the wedding scheduled in two weeks' time, because I did not need to be psychic to see how miserable the life I was going for in this marriage would be. I pulled myself up to my feet, picked up my bag and started walking out, it was for the last time I heard him say, "Come back here. Where do you think you're going?". He kept calling me back.

But it sounded very distant and as remote as I had realized the possibility of a lifetime with this man had become. I opened the door and walked out.

"AKWA EKE"

I got the call at noon, while in the middle of my presentation to our biggest clients and five minutes later, I was in my car reversing out the driveway and heading to the mainland. As I drove out of my parking spot, I hoped and prayed that the new employee who I hurriedly handed off the presentation to was hanging in there, at least. I had set the pace and I had enough material in there that if he only read the screen and ticked off bullet points like an amateur, our clients would remain engaged.

There were some attention-grabbing slides made up of pictures that I had planned to speak over, and I did not know how he would explain those. I imagined him looking lost at the screen as though the pictures would break into an animation and voice over to explain their existence, and that pensive lull that occurs when an unseasoned presenter gives the impression that they are not the authors of the document they are presenting.

The blaring of a noisy, squeaky horn jolted me, and I swerved to avoid being hit by a Keke NAPEP. I shuddered as I noticed that one of the passengers was holding a baby in her arms.

As I zigged and zagged through potholes on lane-less roads, I quickly weighed my options to get to Rumuola Area. I only had about two hours before getting back to the office. If my previous client was important, then the Okoro Consulting Group was huge. This one engagement could represent a third of our business.

I had time, I believed, as I took yet another turn following the transport service bus in front of me with the conductor hanging on the open doorway of the bus and yelling, "Aba! Aba! Aba!", recruiting passengers to the market city, two hours away.

On the original lane that we were on, a car had stopped, and the driver was trying to pop the hissing hood open. We were on the oncoming lane now, but all I could see was traffic, so I followed the ones 'wey sabi road.' I could also hear a police siren in front so I was sure of the shameful comfort of our lane going through as fast as possible. As I navigated the huge bumps caused by erosion, a policeman stepped in front of my car, and I had to brake sharply.

"Oga, why are you driving one-way!" he bellowed.
"You no see other cars for my front?" I responded defensively.
"That one na your business. You are not supposed to go against traffic rules." he responded as he came to my window side while his partner remained standing in front.

I contemplated just ramming into him and going forward but immediately felt some shame in my seething.

"Where are you hurrying to, Oga?" he prompted, seeing I had gone silent.
"I am rushing to go pick my wife. It is urgent."
"Ah, that one is important. Oya, do the needful make Madam no dey wait you. She get belle?"

I realized then that I did not ask the secretary who called me from the meeting for details. She had simply said it was urgent, and I did not think to ask at the time. I had not thought to call my wife because navigating Port Harcourt traffic left no room for phone calls. As I instinctively reached for my phone, the policeman reminded me to hurry up.

“Dem dey wait us for station.” he informed me.

I pulled out a few naira notes along with my iPhone and handed them to the policeman. Too late, I realized the notes were the one-thousand-naira denomination, and I asked him to return two.

“Na my luck na.” the policeman laughed as he waved me on with a half-hearted, “Don’t drive one-way again o.”

I remembered the call that got me here and quickly dialled Sweetie on my phone but after three rings and no answer, I resigned myself to final ten minutes of my drive.

My mind cast to my gorgeous wife, Olamma. Ola, as she was fondly called, means gold. Everyone who sees her takes a second look, and she has that indelible beauty, the type wey dey enter eye. We have been married for two years and if anything, she is even more beautiful now. Her exquisite makeup and diligent styling only enhance her looks. I was enamoured from the moment I met her.

After my aunt introduced us, my mom concurred that this one was a good girl and “knew how to marry”. I was concerned about our ten-year difference, may affect our – I had just turned thirty-five. But my aunty assured me that those were the kind of wives that obeyed their husbands. I laughed while I disagreed in the kind of way that we do when our older relatives dish out well-meaning but misguided advice. It helped that my family liked her; I would not have to do the hard work of convincing them to accept her as their daughter-in-law. It was also a plus that she is smart, funny and a huge boost to my ego.

After we got married, Ola opted to stay home in anticipation for the children, even though she had a degree in business management. Now that I think about it, it had made me feel good to know that someone would be waiting for me at home with delicious cooking and a gorgeous body. It had also felt good to be wanted and *needed*. Yes, that is the word. Ola needs me for money and 'manly' help, as she terms it – she is the cliché damsel-in-distress. She calls me for every and anything.

I glanced back to my phone, and saw she had not called as I turned the final bend and honked at the gate to be let into the apartment complex where we lived. I had an hour to get back to work. So, I jogged to the door, slightly irritated. *Ola should have picked up her phone and been outside waiting for me.* I clanged on the metal door, pacing.

"I'm coming." I heard her respond.
"Hurry up," I said. "What is the matter?"
I kept knocking till Ola opened the door five minutes later, dressed in a floral jumpsuit with her braids packed in a bun; she looked ravishing. As I ran into the bathroom to relieve myself before the journey back to the office, I asked what the matter was.

"Oh, I ran out of cream, and I wanted to quickly get some," she casually mentioned.
"Cream?" I asked incredulously.
"Body lotion." she explained, oblivious to my seething rage.
"I came all the way from Trans Amadi because of cream?" I shouted, rhetorically.
"Sweetie, what did you want me to do now..." she trailed off in her most innocent voice and added somewhat peevishly, "Who else will drive me?"

I noticed the creased lines of her painted lips form a pout.

"I have told you repeatedly to drive the other car I left for you. I even got you a driver who you let go. I cannot be your chauffeur any time you need one. I am busy at work." I said, exasperated but almost pleading.

This is the first time I am protesting this much. At first, I was happy to do her bidding: it had made me feel like a hero and ...

yes... like a man. Who does not want to feel needed? But that was until I realised that it was leaving me in the lurch with regards to my job and my life in general. Then it transitioned from a cute thing to do to an almost manipulative thing. If this compromised my job, then it was not worth the endorphins I felt for being needed so much.

I thought about it some more. It was not just about the job; it was the resentment I was starting to harbour whenever I had to drop everything to be at her beck and call, and the shame I was tempted to feel whenever she said, "But you are the man. Husbands do these things for their wives all the time."

I decided the time had come to take a stand and though still feeling somewhat emasculated, I pleaded with her.

"I can drop you off at the mall but please, use uber when coming back because I will be held up at work until late since I had to take these couple of hours off."

Ola stood in the corner, leaning against the wall, arms folded and pouting, her silhouette the shape of models. She is truly akwaeke- The rare eggs of a python. Ola is beautiful, precious and delicate, one to be taken care of and spent on. This stance always got me losing my voice and sent the blood from my brain somewhere between my legs but not today. There was another vibration down there, it was my phone in my pocket and I knew it was the office.

“Pretty, please? ”I walked up to her and mouthed.

She dropped her arms and looked in my eyes, and I felt her large brown eyes swallowing me in that uncanny way. “Oya, let’s be going now,” she said.

“I mean it, Ola. I won’t be able to pick you up if I dropped you off now,” I reiterated.

She took her small purse beside her and sashayed to the door. To be honest, I did not think this would end amicably. Ola did not like to be denied or refused anything. Her word was law in this house; her sultry and pouty words, not the demanding tone anyone would have suspected from a controlling wife. I knew what consequences awaited me if I did not do her bidding.

We walked to the car and drove to the mall. Before she dropped off, she gave me a full kiss on the lips and said, “Thank you, Darling.”

Oh, the rush I feel every time I please her and she rewards me with these kisses or even a smile! I hated to break the spell, but I had to remind her. “I will be in meetings. Please, get a taxi when you are done.”

“See you later Darling,” She said in response, as she placed a dainty, polished finger on my nose before she started making her way out of the car.

“I mean it, Ola. I’m not joking.”

As she walked away, her legs barely touching the ground, I noticed how people were already taking second glances, captivated by her beauty and endowment.

By the time I meandered through traffic and got back to the office, my clients had gone, even though I spent half my drive over on the phone, using every trick I could think up to keep them waiting until I arrived. Not only had my counterpart at the other company come, he had come with his CEO to tour our facilities as well. This is bad for business. Very bad! I went to meet them over at their hotel. I pulled all the stops to get a meeting room at the hotel and put on my best show to present after I whet their appetite with fine dining and wining, all-expense paid by our company, of course.

“Family emergency.” I responded when they asked where I had been.

But the words felt puny to me, and I resolved never to have to make that excuse again. Before I started my presentation, my phone started ringing. It was Ola. It had been a couple of hours so I suspected she had made her way back. I quickly took the call.

“I’ve been calling you—” she started.
“I’m sorry Baby. I am with my clients.” I apologised,
“I’m done at the mall. Please, come and take me home,” she said. I was so shocked that I did not respond. “Are you there?” she asked.
“Ola, I told you I will not be able to take you back home. Why are you doing this? You promised.”

She said she never promised anything and asked that I hurry as it was getting dark; and I knew that this was not going to end except I ended it.

“Ola, you are going to have to find your way home. I am not coming for you today.”

As I hung up, I heard her protests but I turned off my phone and went into the conference room to deliver my presentation on the benefits of using an auditing firm that is experienced in taxation, litigation, and accounting. Thankfully, my clients were engaged and asking questions. You know you have them when they start articulating some new benefits they see in your organisation and explaining possible scenarios for collaboration.

Amid this, my assistant reached into the room and asked for a minute. I asked him to come and he whispered in my ears that Ola had called thrice, saying it was an emergency.

"Don't disturb me during this presentation for any reason," I said, smiling. As he looked at me perplexed, I asked for confirmation. "Did you hear what I said?"
"Yes, sir." he mouthed and left the room.

Suffice to say, we got the business, and I was surer than ever that I should honour my commitments in future.

When I got back that night, she was already home. She cussed me out with all the phrases that used to move me; I did not care about her, I left her by herself in the dark at night. She is my wife, did I not know that? She asked, before reminding me that I was supposed to take care of her.

I responded with the reasoning that doing my job effectively and keeping my commitments was taking care of her. Then, I asked her to give it some thought, but nothing I said seemed to move her. Instead, the explanations seemed to fuel her anger, so I let her be. I did not beg, as usual. I only apologised for her discomfort and asked how I could help her feel better. That only served to infuriate her some more.

It was a difficult couple of weeks after that day with Olamma giving me the silent treatment and making exaggerated stomps around the house, but I resolved to do nothing about it, especially as I noticed that she was beginning to do things for herself. It was validating...it was progress. Sometimes, I wished to be her knight in shining armour but I had broken through that. She is a full-grown adult. I respected her, so I will not treat her like a child who needs rescuing and saving.

After three weeks of torture – and answering to my aunty who she also reported me to, we both knew where we stood. I also began to understand her fear to stand on her own two feet and repeat the examples she saw growing up. We are in a better place now. I am no longer called for outrageous 'emergencies' and Ola has started driving herself, as she should. We have grown even though it didn't come easy.

MONEY MATTERS

The pressure inside her was building as she hung up the phone. She had to leave the hospital before she exploded. She took a deep breath and braced herself to smile on her walk through the pristine hospital hallway, past the Nurses' station where she bade the incoming shift goodbye and then waved at the difficult billionaire heiress in Room 706. The pressure was mounting, but she made it to the lobby downstairs, where she encountered half of the 'Nigerian Nurses Association' leadership: Omobola from Ekiti, Tejiri from Warri and Akunna from Nnewi.

They stopped to remind her of yet another wake keep for the grand aunt of a fellow Nigerian nurse, a child's graduation and the associated contribution, for each. When she seemed unsure, they said they would resend the transfer details, so she could send money via zelle or cash app.

By now, the smile she had plastered on her face was threatening to crack. But it was she: the nice agreeable Nwakaego, who would give her all for the good of community, and others. They had crowned her Florence Nightingale on her floor at the hospital and in the church where her selfless service extended to.

The ladies asked after her husband as usual. Today, she struggled to get out the usual, "He's fine o." Her response always while beaming with pride, because being married was one of her greatest achievements. In fact, these days, staying married as a Nigerian nurse in Houston was regarded as saintly and commendable. She knew how to keep her home.

She could not think of a greater achievement. No matter the cost, staying married was becoming almost impossible, so for her, the respectful glances people, especially colleagues sent her way was all she needed. She knew too that this had been responsible for some awards she had been given by the church.

As she continued her way to the parking garage, she was on autopilot.

The phone call she had just received was from Nigeria where her family lived. Her brother, Nnamdi had called her to let her know that her mother had gone from needing surgery to requiring dialysis twice every week.

She was too shocked and in disbelief to process the only explanation to what Nnamdi was saying: she had sent more than was needed for Mama's surgery and timely too. There was only one person who had some explaining to do and he was the reason for this terrible state. She had come undone and was afraid to confront the ugly truth that would puncture holes in their beautiful castle.

She jolted out of her contemplation as she took in the flash of colors from the many cars parked at the garage. Her steps had become even heavier. She located her Toyota Rav 4 and stepped into the vehicle. She started it so the air conditioner could ward off the relentless Houston heat.

Then she broke down and let out a piercing scream. She wept and cried as hot tears ran freely down her face; washing the

Mary Kay brown powder, the only make-up she wore, with it and making a mess of her blue medical scrubs.

Her heart was wrenching in that way that was slow and excruciating. The betrayal she felt was beyond what had happened. All the while thinking, "Who do I turn to when the person who is supposed to be closest to me is the one hurting me?"

She was sad, distraught and needed answers. Her brother had called to say Mama's kidney had failed. And they were putting the surgery on hold to tend to the more urgent procedure of dialysis. He said the surgery was delayed because they could not come up with the money required.

"Sister Nwakaego, there is no money o, we haven't received any money."

"What do you mean? Today is Thursday. I sent it way ahead of time so that you will get it before it is needed." Nwakaego interjected.

"What do you mean? Why haven't they done the surgery? Did the money get there late?"

"What money, Sister?" Nnamdi had asked confusedly.

"The money I sent since Monday. Today is Thursday; I sent it way ahead of time so you will get it."

Nnamdi's stuttering had confirmed her fears. "Sister Nwakaego, there is no money o. I did not receive any alert.

How did you send it? Did you use Western Union"?
As he was asking, a foreboding came upon her. She had asked Cheta to send the $ 3,000 dollars: enough for the surgery, medicine and any other associated expenses. "Don't worry, Nnamdi... let me sort it out. *Ka m kpo gi, inu?*"

She shivered at his last words before he dropped the call rang piercingly through her ears, "It's not looking good, Sister..."

She knew the hospital would not consider the surgery till they had the full amount. Mama's doctor at the teaching hospital, who was also the co-owner of her own private hospital, had told her. Especially because she had tried to bring consultants from the teaching hospital to perform the surgery with her at the private hospital Mama was now in. They all had to be paid.

They no longer took her mom to the teaching hospital, because of the power failure during her last procedure for hours. Thankfully, it had been a minor surgery, but others had harrowing tales of how there were no emergency backup generators. Also, several people from their hometown, who had come to the city for routine treatment, had died without explanation.

Many of the egghead professor doctors there had their own private hospitals or spent much of their time consulting at one. So, it was one of the residents who had advised Nnamdi to register Mama at one of those hospitals saying, "At least, you have people abroad that can pay, okwaya?"

And that's how Mama had been attending one of the professor's clinic in Port Harcourt, where she regularly received treatment. However, 'No Pay-No Treatment' is a binding policy in these hospitals, including the teaching hospitals. In emergency cases like childbirth, mother and child were literally held ransom like prisoners until the bill was paid, which would never happen in America where patients were discharged almost like a revolving door to free up bed space. The process was even faster in cases where patients had no insurance.

All these complexities were what made her even more upset that the cog in the wheel was her own husband. When Mama fell ill, she had to ask for extra overtime shift to quickly make enough money to send. No, she did not have savings especially since Cheta started his business. Make that his latest business. The last eight years had been one business after another, with Nwakaego in the role of founder.

After talking with her brother that morning, perplexed and with a deep sense of foreboding, she knew but she wanted to wish the knowing away. The possibility that her husband could likely be responsible, for this travesty. But she called anyways.

"Babe, Nnamdi called to say they have not received the money."
"Hello Babe," he responded coolly.
"Did you send it through the African store? Or through Western Union?" she asked, giving him options, delaying the inevitable.
Silence.

"Cheta, are you there?"
"I am... when you come home now..." He was stalling and she could sense it.
"What do you mean when I come home? Mama needs it now. If you haven't sent it, please send it quickly. Things are getting bad fast."
He responded, "I said when you come home, we will discuss, why are you waking me up and shouting this morning?"

He was using intimidation and that had always worked. But this time, it was different for Nwakaego. Maybe because it was her mother's life on the line or she had had enough, she didn't care which it was. A new stirring was beginning to boil up in her and it caused her to speak up, her voice rising formidably.

“Where IS the money?” her tone was different, both firm and loud.

This time he answered the question. “Uncle called me that they needed some money to complete the foundation as the rains are coming soon. I’m going to send Mama’s money. I’m expecting some money...” he trailed off cluelessly

That was what broke the dam. Nwakaego started yelling and hurling the insults,
“My own mother? My sick mother’s money is what you took. You are a useless man! How could you? Which money are you expecting from where? From your failed or imaginary businesses?”

She would have continued but what was the point? And she was exhausted, on her way out after a 12-hour night shift. She hung up the phone, took a deep breath and reclined her seat. All energy had left her.

As she sobbed quietly in her prostrate state, she remembered how it all started. She had studied nursing at Umuahia

in Eastern Nigeria. She was graduating with an Ordinary National Diploma, the equivalent of an associate degree at twenty-four when her family met some "abroad-returnees" in the village at an event. It could have been a funeral, a wedding or maybe an August meeting for women, she could not tell now.

His family had said Cheta was looking for a wife. A good born-again Christian and someone in the medical field preferably a doctor, a pharmacist or a nurse. Her aunty had promptly mentioned Nwakaego, who for good measure, added that she was from a good family and her dad was a clergyman. She promised to get back with them and then called to tell her parents. Of course, they were interested, but hesitantly so because they wanted to be sure he was the real deal: 'a good boy with a good job'.

So Cheta's uncle had come to Umuahia to visit Nwakaego's parents and allay any concerns they may have. When he heard they were her parents, he had said this one will 'know how to marry' code phrase for subservient and hapless.

When her parents called to ask her, she was excited and interested. Her only concern was his faith. And they had told her he was a good Christian. All her classmates were beginning to get married or engaged in final year of school. It was the dream: study hard, marry, and get a job. Even if you got a job before getting married, the wedding was expected to be in the works.

No one ever told Nwakaego about the professional preference. Nor would she have understood why. Since coming to Houston, she had since learned why. One of the highest paid associate or bachelor's degree entry level jobs in America is nursing. With a degree from Nigeria, one only had to take the board exams to start earning.

When they just started talking on the phone, Cheta had a job as a Corrections Officer at the Prison Service in America. They got along well, and she started having feelings for him. A few months later, his uncle and family came to her house to do the introduction. Both his parents had passed on. He had come to Nigeria six months later, and they had done the Igba Nkwu traditional ceremony at the family home and the white wedding in church.

He returned alone after filing her papers in Lagos to get a green card as his wife. It was a happy, fun time and they had the newly-wed glow. Everything seemed to be working out and she was sad to see him go. But he seemed on top of things with all the documents required and he assured her the permanent residency would be granted in no time.

In that month he was in Nigeria, she had gotten pregnant and seven months after her wedding, she was granted permanent residency. This was just in time for their first child to be born in the US. It was the first time she was boarding a plane. The whole experience was surreal, but the promise of a new life felt like walking on clouds. Their baby was born without issues four weeks after she arrived and she and Cheta fit well into the roles of new parents, doting on little Aham.

While baby was nursing, she studied for and passed her boards. Cheta was the best husband during this period, supporting her with a boot camp for the boards and helping at home while she studied, taking care of the baby. She passed after two attempts because oyibo patient-focused nursing was somewhat different than what she was used to. He had encouraged her, dutifully waking her up at night to go study. She was impressed by his love and lived for those days.

Soon she was applying for jobs. Rather, they both were applying for jobs because sometimes she would get an email that said, "Thank you for applying for such and such a role." She knew he loved her and wanted the best for her, so she was glad.

Then she got an interview for a doctor's office. The schedule was for eight to four. And she thought it would be good to have a schedule that allowed her drop and pick the baby from day care since Cheta was out of town for three to four days at a time at his corrections officer job in Huntsville Prisons, two hours away.

"You should turn it down." was her husband's response to her offer. Perplexed, she persisted and put forth all the great reasons for work- life balance she had considered, but he preferred the hospitals. She has since found out that the reasons he liked the 12-hour shifts that only hospitals gave were because of the overtime pay, which was easy to rack up with such long hours.

Like the faithful and resourceful wife she was, she went to work for her family. A full-time job of three shifts to make the 40 hours requirements was now a mirage. She easily worked six days a week now.

Cheta was exploring a business venture: more like he was committing and spending on business ideas. He said he needed the money to 'fail and fail fast' so he could prove his concept, like his life coach had said. So many coaches he had as well: one for business finance, another for online marketing, even one for mindset, yet another for branding. And he never did group coaching; he always went for tailored one on one session because according to him, 'premium coaching gave premium results.'

And spend they did, while he focused full time on business. Cheta would say entrepreneurship was the way to go for young black males in America to spread the wealth in black America. That they were not just going to be rich, they would be 'moving the needle on racial equity'.

Nwakaego was daily inspired in the early days; Cheta was quite the smooth talker. And he watched several 'powerful' speakers on YouTube. And he spewed the motivation:

"Life will not work unless you work it."
"What would you do if you knew you could not fail?"
"Fear is a mirage."

But when even-keeled Nwakaego would wonder about jobs and stability, Cheta would give his standard example of success: Richard Branson and Steve Jobs who pursued their own dreams at the risk of their careers. All he needed, he said was a woman who believed enough in his dreams to help him reach for the stars. And so, he quit his Correction Officer Job saying the "good in his hand was the enemy of his possible best."

The trouble was this best had remained a potential. It had been three long years with one failed business venture after another. Cheta would not call them failures. He would say they were valuable lessons; as he claimed, they had taught him what not to do in business.

It took her another dutiful two years to see through the facade. She thought they had been saving some money apart from the family's welfare and his business ventures. Her salary, all she made went into their joint account. But he was primarily in charge of the budget and disbursed as necessary. He was also sending 15% to a savings account, he said.

At this point, she was constantly exhausted. A second pregnancy had given them a beautiful daughter, and another day care cost. Yes, both kids went there as Cheta said he needed to be mobile to pursue business leads. Only for a little while, she would encourage herself holding on to the lures of the American dream.

At work, she would hear tales of Nigerian nurses and the myth of their wealth. The thought was that they earned tons of money and garnered overtime like no man's business. They rumored that these women were stubborn and rebellious to their men. Jezebels wanting to wear the pants in the marriage and prone to abandon the men who had rescued them from whatever hole they crawled out of, to a bright future in the US of A.

Divorce was way too common, and she heard many instances of domestic violence as things got to a head. She noticed these divorced female nurses were mostly married to the 'dreamers' and not the typical 'working' husbands. As a result, she committed to getting hers right. She would support her husband and protect their marriage, no matter the cost. Also, she noticed he was always so nice to her, so long as the money kept coming in. So she kept going out to work more shifts and more jobs.

And work she did, till she found out there were no savings when her father died. Before then, she trusted him infinitely. For the funeral, the Umunna of her hometown had sent a long list, of requirements for burial rites, to Cheta, the VIP in-law who was married to Papa's Ada.

It ran into thousands of dollars, and it only made sense to come from the savings she believed he had been building from the money her long and tiring shifts had racked up. That was when he has started with the excuses. He had invested it in some quick scheme, and it was going to mature in another three months. They could not pull it out prematurely. He didn't want to leave the money in the account because "money that wasn't gaining interest is money that is reducing in value."

It was the first time she started noticing the chink in his armor. The feeling was unsettling. It made her think beneath his words on the surface to deduce the meaning and implication. She never used to do that, question him in her mind like that. And she chided herself a little for it. She figured she would reason with him to pull out the investment. But he persuaded her to work a few more hours to make up the money. They deserved to have their savings intact for their family stability he had explained.

She did not even have a retirement fund like her colleagues did in 401K investments. Cheta said that was the government's slow way of holding your money ransom with the promise of a 'small interest' he said he could do better at trading with the money. Moreover, they were going to be rich and not be at the mercy of government inflation and conservative investment practices. Clearly, government was no good at managing money like Cheta would.

She had worked alternating days of six shifts a week. Before the funeral she worked a gruelling ten-day shift before traveling to Nigeria for the burial of her late father. She was so fatigued; she slept through the 13-hour direct flight from Houston to Lagos. Of course, she also gave Cheta the money he sent to his uncle to fulfil the traditional in-laws list for the funeral. Thankfully, everything went relatively well barring the extortionist behavior of her relatives and community leaders.

However, when the three months maturity reached, Cheta could still not come up with the money. In addition, his uncle had been putting pressure on him, to build a house in the village. He said, others were encroaching on his inheritance. And unless he fenced the land, it was vulnerable to the Lagos boys who were stealing other people's lands by a few feet here and there. Nwakaego tried to talk him out of being too hasty, saying whenever the investment matured; Cheta could use some of it.

Her voice was getting stronger now. She felt they both owned this decision unlike before, when she would leave it all up to him to decide. She was beginning to take an interest in the bank account now. She still saw large amounts leave, but he said it was for business. At least, all the bills were paid.

There was this time even the electricity had been cut off. Cheta had complained about the American system that did not honor loyalty. He even asked if they needed cable so he could further reduce the amount of outgoing bills. She was going to have her little luxuries where she could get them.

Emphatically, she refused for the cable or the internet to be cut.

She hated to be one of the other nurses who would not support their husband's dreams. But she had asked him recently, if he would start applying for jobs, pending his big break in business. He did not speak to her for a week, claiming she did not understand. He expected his wife of all people to be his pillar through this journey. And that she did not have the stamina or faith to marry a visionary. Could she not see that a breakthrough was imminent?

The money she thought was going towards a down payment on their own home had become elusive. She had no hope that it would resurface from whatever investment whole he had placed it since her dad died and her mom took ill, she had been sending money to Nigeria more frequently. Cheta had asked her to slow down because "the more you give, the more they want."

That was one of the few times she had snapped at him, "This is my mother we are talking about. Don't tell me that."
He had grumbled but he had been making the transfer, faithfully.

He was still making the case for the house in his village. By now the fencing was completed they had been sending monies in manageable portions. But he wanted to pay bulk money for the building which they did not have to spare, without compromising their welfare or making Nwakaego work herself to death.

On the phone when she had confronted him after her brother's call, he had said a man of his stature at forty years should have a house in his village. He actually questioned why she did not see that. These were the words that were hurting her deeply now. This was the betrayal. It was all about him. It had always been all about him. Her, having his children. Her, funding his business. And now her building his house. She was sold a dream of 'theirs' And now she knew that even if the pie-in-the-sky business had thrived, it would be his success. And no, she was not okay with that.

The hot tears and the deep groans came from a depth within her: grieving what was and remained a dream, producing a clear realization of what she had to do next. She could not change him, but she could change herself. She could plan for those two children. And the new one she just found out she was carrying, due in thirty-three weeks.

She had no retirement contribution in her 401k, no college fund for the children, no money to take care of her sick mother, with four years of earning over a hundred thousand dollars annually. What had she toiled for? A nightmare? a dream? She was going to choose them and do what she should have done a long time ago.

In making that decision, she realized she had chosen herself first. The feeling was as strange as it was liberating. The tears that came now were not the hot burning tears of hurt. They were the cleansing flood for her soul, welcoming the new Nwakaego. The one that did not have to enable her husband to have a happy home. She would own her responsibility and entertain no excuses for it. She would not let the fear of divorce and shame into every decision she made.

The path appeared clear before her and she would walk in it. She was going to open a new bank account for her pay, where only she had access till Cheta could earn her trust again. She would contribute to her pension fund and retirement account and take advantage of her hospital's match to maximize her investment.

She would take yet another loan to send for her mom's medical bills. She would catch up on all payments and be consistent with the many loans taken out for more ideas than she could remember. And she would not enable or condone financial impropriety going forward. She would be honest with her opinions. He seemed to like the hard truth that came from the coaches, maybe her candor could help him be more objective and possibly, successful.

She would have this conversation when she got home. She did not know what he would say. But she knew he would not be pleased. That was okay. She could not feel his feelings for him or own them anymore. She said a word of prayer and was enveloped by a calm and peace she had not felt in a while.

The SUV started with a purr then a roar as she pulled out the parking lot, face puffy from crying. But with definite clarity and direction in her eyes, she drove to the bank to make it all happen.

Nwakaego's mother lived another eight years and she could afford the caregiver and medical care she needed till the end. It was a rocky three months afterwards but Nwakaego remained resolute. They attended a Finance & Legacy two-month long class and marriage counseling. This was the best thing that could have happened to them. Cheta ranted and threatened about access to the funds but eventually, got a job at the bank and a side business as a realtor. He still talks big but at least, he gets a paycheck every month.

THE PROPHET

The persistent piercing sound from the ringing phone jolted Adiagha back to the present. These daytime dreams, or were they nightmares, had become more frequent since the last episode.

She hurried from the bed to the bathtub where eucalyptus mingled with the ever-refreshing vanilla scents held a promise of rejuvenating and relaxing her nerves.

One glance at the phone and she saw it was her Aunty Uyai. But she had inadvertently picked the call; she mentally kicked herself as she cut it. Before she could catch a breath, Aunty was calling back: better prepared this time, Adiagha calmly scrolled up to the automated reply messages and selected "at a meeting, will call you back."

She let herself enjoy a chuckle; yes, she was at a meeting. A come-to-Jesus meeting with her ovaries, soaking in an essential oil infused warm bath. As she slid back into the soothing water, the creases on her brows returned.

The house was quiet, as Bassey had gone to work. She had gone through the routine with him, getting ready for work, he would make her a cup of coffee for her hour-long commute and she would give him the full kiss on the lips before they walked to their cars and drove off.

Only this time, she had made a U-turn after ten minutes and driven back home. She had cancelled her morning meetings and updated her automatic replies to say tending to "a family emergency". An emergency it was, they were approaching their 7th wedding anniversary and still no cry of a baby in their home.

They had met as students at the University of Glasgow in Scotland. It was meant to be. In a city where English sounded like a cross between Dutch and Anang language, they were two single Nigerians attending the same church and in the same faculty. After their master's degrees in economics and business administration, they had found jobs and gotten married in the architectural beauty that was the Church of Scotland on Buchanan Street.

With their distinctions and two-year post study visa, it was not difficult to get jobs at the investment banks in Glasgow's downtown. The first two years of their marriage had been a breeze, they journeyed Europe as a couple from the ruins of Greece to the cuisine of Italy. They toured and travelled. Their concerns in those days were which new city or village to visit and moving up in their jobs. They chased career and had big dreams.

The path was to have their company eventually file for permanent residency in the United Kingdom. However, when the new Tory government came in, they ended the post study visa that allowed international students to work after graduation. They had a choice: to return for a PhD just to maintain status or to return to Nigeria.

This was not the dream but they had no choice in the matter. Thankfully, Nigerian banks were hiring and the couple were swooped up when they applied. It was quite the transition. Now they are back home and living so close to family.

At first it was delightful, seeing the family and her in-laws quite often and being fawned over as the 'new wife' until the questions started coming. At first it was prayers, "Our wife, see as you fine... that's how beautiful your babies will be too, in Jesus name." Then the assumptions followed, "This one you are shining like this, this looks like pregnancy glow o."

Clearly, as a new wife, one could not even admit sickness or discomfort; else they would share those winks and start counting down the nine-month calendar. It was the same inference drawn for any semblance of weight: "you're adding weight o. I like it."

Others would tease the newly wed woman saying that oga is a sharp shooter and she a correct goalkeeper by mere assumption.

Those did not quite bother her till her mother-in-law started asking her own brand of questions:

"What is happening o? You people should give me my grandchildren please."
"Bassey you are my first son, I don't want your father's people to laugh at me please."

It was funny how she always made it about her. After almost forty years of marriage, she still had something to prove with her own in-laws. In the early days, Adiagha would follow with "We are trying Ma. Don't worry, God will answer us."

Bassey would not even bother. The doctor had told them everything was fine with them, to keep trying and to not stress about it.

Easier said than done, the pressure was not an option in Nigeria where brides seemed to easily produce babies after nine months. Several of them had quick succession pregnancies. In church, the last Sunday of the month was for dedication of babies and they came in their droves. It was getting hard to participate especially when couples whose weddings they had just attended in the same year, came to dedicate their babies. Seemingly, her mother-in-law was feeling the pressure as well. Adiagha did not understand why though, Bassey had two other sisters who had five children between them. Surely they kept her busy and fulfilled. But no, not producing a grandchild who bore her husband's name had become a personal challenge for Mama.

It was on their fourth wedding anniversary she summoned Adiagha to her house for an urgent meeting, that Friday evening.

"Adiagha, come to the house by 6pm ehn. There is somewhere I want to take you."
"Oh, Mama, Bassey will still be at work, when he comes back, we will come around 7pm." Adiagha replied, calmly bidding her exasperation.
She was surprised when Mama responded, "No, just you, not Bassey."

And so she went, curiosity piqued but not particularly alarmed. She had began to avoid any meeting with Mama for obvious reasons.

When Adiagha arrived, she found her waiting on the front porch, clutching her purse and pacing, dressed in white. As she greeted her, Mama responded, "What are you wearing?"

Adiagha did a double take. Why, she was in jeans and a tee shirt, what was wrong with it?

"You have to change. Come inside. We have to hurry."
"Ah, Ma where are we going?"

Mama's silence was the only response she got. She went into the room and came back out with an adire boubou- a free-flowing kaftan and a headscarf.

"Wear this. We are going to church. You have to look respectable. You are a married woman."
"Oh Ma, Bassey and I are supposed to go out for dinner this evening."
"What dinner are you having? What is there to celebrate when there is no cry of a baby in that house? Don't you want children? You and Bassey are still doing like boyfriend and girlfriend? Look, my daughter, you are a married woman. It is a woman that builds her home. Let this pastor pray for you and open your womb."

Adiagha was momentarily stunned. The words were like daggers to her. She wanted to explain and defend but she decided against it, walked into the guestroom and changed her clothes as Mama had instructed. Her own family had shown concern but were understandably kinder. The honeymoon was over.

That day at the church with Mama still remained indelible in her mind. It was not a typical church building; it was more like a doctor's office with paraphernalia hanging on the walls as they waited in the lobby. Mama went to speak to the lady at the desk as she looked around. On the wall hung a massive frame of a man in the same way the president's photo hung in the lobby of corporate buildings.

What curdled her blood were his titles, it read *"Prophet Jehoshaphat Emmanuel, Demon Chaser and Witch Killer".* He looked menacing, with a red cape over his shoulders like superman about to fly, but his eyes seemed to be peering disapprovingly at her. She turned away.

Faintly, she could hear people praying and chanting. A woman came out of the prayer room, went up to the receptionist and handed her some money, in return she gave her a bottle that Adiagha made out to be the popular brand of olive oil. Her next steps terrified Adiaha. She walked to the photo on the wall, opened the bottle and dabbed the oil on her forehead muttering, "Thank you Prophet." Thrice she did this, each time bowing to the photo. Then she walked out of the building. Adiagha squirmed in her seat. She glanced at her mother-in-law who sat with a determined look in her eyes and her mouth set in a firm line. The receptionist turned to herself and her mother-in-law and said, "The prophet will see you next."

Prophet Jehoshaphat looked exactly as he did in the photograph. Towering and menacing, he did not smile and had his eyes set intently on her belly. As Mama started to greet him, he raised his hand sharply and remained fixated on Adiaha's abdomen. He started to mutter something unintelligible between shouts of "I see! I see!" They remained rooted to the spot. Finally he moved towards her, she gave a start and stepped back. She felt Mama shove her forward.

With his face barely 6 inches from hers, he started speaking with a loud voice, splattering saliva on her face, "I see the enemy of your progress, she is a woman who has tied your womb."

Mama let out a shout "Oh Jesuuuusss !"
He looked at her sternly and instructed, "Be quiet woman!"
She covered her mouth with one hand but Adiaha could still hear her whimpering.

He continued in his foreboding voice, "But that is not the only issue. The bottle. Yes the bottle. The bottle she tied your womb in she has taken to keep in the coven with all the other witches."

Mama's whimpering was getting louder with each announcement. Adiagha dutifully stayed in line, wondering if she were on a Nollywood movie set. But this was real, there was a man telling her these things.

He continued "If this woman had the womb with her, I could have handled the matter speedily but now it is in the hands of the coven and they are guarding it."

"Prophet, please help us..." Mama was saying.
He held a hand up again and Mama stopped.
"Who is doing this to you?" He asked Adiagha. She thought

he was being rhetorical but he asked again, louder this time. “I don’t know, sir.” Answered a bewildered Adiagha.

He brooded a bit and said, “We will soon find out. When you come on your next visit we will know. Before then, I will go to the mountain to fast and pray with a company of prophets. I will give you a list of prayers to pray and oil to anoint yourself everyday.”

Finally, he turned to her mother-in-law, “This is the difficult type but there is nothing God cannot do. You will have to triple the payment. I am just helping you because what I see coming to this your daughter...” he paused ominously and shook his head.

Mama thanked him profusely and scurried with her out of the room to the receptionist. Adiagha had seen her hand over bundles of naira notes to the lady. She had seen enough and walked out to the car to wait for her mother-in-law. When she eventually came, she said, “you did not thank the prophet. Next time we come, you will do as that woman: you anoint yourself with the oil and say *thank you* three times. The receptionist said it works like magic.”

After handing Adiaha the oil and the prayer book, she outlined the many instructions on times of day she should anoint herself and pray as well as specific postures to take. She had become her exuberant self again, like someone whose hope had been restored. She was thanking God for deliverance as they drove home, cursing the devil and his coven of witches. Staring out of the car in the distance, Adiagha wondered if the experience was real.

That was a year ago. Bassey had wondered where she went when she returned. He did not understand why she went with his mother. They were so oblivious, these husbands, never realising the pressure wives feel to gratify their mothers-in-laws. Why would they? Their mums let them get away with everything while they judge their daughters-in-law at the slightest infraction.

She had ignored his advice and gone back with her mother-in-law one more time to see the prophet. After extending his supposed time at the mountain, demanding more money to unveil the identity of the woman who had tied her children in the spirit realm, he summoned them to hear the good news. "Good news indeed!" That had made her laugh and some soapsuds overflowed the bathtub. She steadied herself as her head soaked in her thoughts again.

At this meeting, he said it was Adiaha's sister who was responsible for the evil of this infertility. Adiagha started, "But Prophet..."

He held up that stern hand again and continued, "I know! Who would believe that somebody who came out of the same mother's womb could do you like this? Human beings are very wicked. And your sister is very strong in the spirit realm. I and the other prophets are going back to the mountain to fight her. She will die before she knows what is happening..."

Adiagha could not hold it in any longer, "But Prophet, I don't have a sister!" she exclaimed.

She noticed that Mama had stopped chanting the "Jesus, Jesus" that she had been responding to his every word since they came into the office.

Prophet Jehoshaphat looked momentarily taken aback but he regained himself quickly, "Are you calling me a liar? There is a woman. Maybe she is not your sister but she is close to you... ehm, she is short, no medium height... a little light skinned but more like chocolate complexion..."

Adiagha had heard enough; she turned on her heels and walked out his office. She heard her mother in-law apologising to the prophet and calling out to her, but she kept walking to the car.

This weekend would be their seventh anniversary. In the last year, she had seen her parents go from concerned to wary of mentioning the issue. Yes, the inability of her marriage to produce children was an issue. Her mother-in-law had reported to Bassey about how she refused to go for special prayers. The matter was a spiritual one, she told him. Her enemies were at work, she said, but she assured him that she knew mighty prophets that will put them to shame. All mama needed was the couple's cooperation; after all, "What an adult could see sitting down, a child cannot see standing up." ... Her usual talk.

He used to tell her these things. They would laugh as they shared their family gossip and the preposterous things Nigerian elders are wont to say. But not anymore, Bassey was not quite telling her anything nowadays. That was how she knew Mama was getting to him.

After the last doctor's visit and three failed rounds of invitro fertilisation, they started considering surrogacy and adoption. Mama condemned the idea of another woman carrying her grandchild. The last two adoption opportunities that came,

Mama had said the children were witches and the devil was trying to bring them in our home. It was Aunty Uyai who had found the young university student who got accidentally pregnant and wanted to give up the child. Was life not funny? Someone else's accident was going to be her miracle. Now she dreaded returning Aunty Uyai's call, she would feel she was not serious about the adoption.

Bassey said he did not want the baby anymore and they should wait for God's time. She could not pretend to carry on as usual, going to work and coming back home, when all she wanted was a baby. But no one else seemed to see that: not Aunty Uyai, not Mama, not her parents, God bless their hearts and now, not even Bassey. She could feel the distance growing between them.

At their anniversary dinner this weekend, she would have a heart to heart conversation with him. It felt like there was a wedge between them. What was sure was that they both wanted a baby and Bassey would have to decide on the routes they could take to get there: surrogacy or adoption.

She felt better already and hopeful as she stepped out of the tub. Maybe they would go back to the couple that told each other everything and were on the same page. Maybe they would finally have a baby she could cradle in her arms. Maybe then, this cloud that seemed to sap her energy and zest for life would lift. What if it never lifted? Then she must accept that she was enough and make the most of the rest of her life, with the man who loved her.

SUSPICION

When everything was quiet, I knew she was going through my phone again. I was in the adjacent bathroom, and I had heard her soliloquizing. I sighed and shook my head, taking my time to towel myself more leisurely. The mist on the mirror clouded my image, slowly obscuring my view. That's how I felt about my marriage. We were closer than ever before in terms of proximity, but farther in spirit and in clarity.

I had spent these last two years of newly-wed life: convincing, defending and proving myself to Tariela: my wife, my African

Queen. Such was her striking beauty that people often mistook her for a model. God blessed her with extra melanin, the type people meant when they said, 'your black dey shine.'

And they would ask "Blackie, are you from Ghana?" When she said no, they would ask, "Sierra Leone?" and a couple other guesses would follow. But when she would ultimately reveal, that she was from Ijaw, in South- South Nigeria, nods and sounds of affirmation would follow with most affirming,

"Na true o. Una black dey shine." It is well known that the Ijaws are some of the darker skinned ethnic group in Nigeria. Even then, some black shone, while others were classified 'dirty'. In this case, oily skin was a plus.

It is this gorgeous lady that I am married to. Her qualities were skin deep. She had the brains to match her beauty. Graduating top of her class at the Niger Delta University in Business Management, she was working at a foremost consulting firm. When we first met, we were both in choir at The Refiners' Church in Yenagoa, Bayelsa State. I had just moved to the city on a developmental project manager assignment for UNDP, building and stocking maternity centres in the Niger Delta. As an idealist willing to risk a cushy career for social impact,

I was well in my element. Putting in long hours and having a devout sense of service was evident in my work ethic.

Beyond project work and pressing deadlines, my only recourse was my faith. I remained committed to a local assembly in the area. And my penchant for playing musical instruments led me to the choir.

A single, hardworking brother who had a job was a scarce commodity and is highly sought after by single ladies in church. Sisters who have been seeking their 'Boaz', to quote the cliché titles of the singles outreach programmes that many attended faithfully and fervently.

I knew several ladies were interested in me. It was becoming a normal occurrence for me. Sad that they were not many men in church who were devout and had a career or business. No wonder it always seemed like there was a scarcity of men. It was not scarcity of quantity. It was one of quality. But I did not let it get to my head. I remained humble and helpful, showing up for rehearsals and helping with individual voice coaching afterwards.

I was a long way from my home state in Nassarawa outside Abuja, Federal Capital Territory of Nigeria, where I bagged my degree in Social Work. I knew from a young age that I wanted to serve Nigeria to make social impact. All it would take, my young mind thought, were passion, hard work, and an undying heart of service. That was why I went to Yenagoa.

Inadvertently, I carried this everywhere I went and communicated to everyone I interacted with. Anyway, I digress, but that was the spirit with which I served the sisters in church. I never thought I was strict just that I was doing my best to build them up in the faith and train their voices.

Unknown to me, many of the ladies had started laying claim to me, warding others off me, spreading rumours that I was attracted to them. If I had known earlier, I would have practiced better boundaries around them. But I naively thought I was just a friend, till the day I met Tariela.

The first time she came to church. I was enamoured. It was the kind of face you saw once and could never un-see. My mind took a snapshot and hung the photo at its front door. I thought about her throughout the week. I had only sighted her from the stage, while I was on the piano.

Imagine my delight when she came into choir rehearsal the following week. Before long, we hit it off and started dating. I wanted to do things right, so I spoke to our pastor. That's when I first heard the other woman. Apparently, several sisters had given the impression that we were dating. When Pastor mentioned who he thought I was interested in, I was in shocked. It took some convincing for him to believe me and support our relationship.

By this time, Tariela had started getting cold shoulder in the choir; the gossip was that she was an upstart who came to reap where she did not sow. She would cry and blame me for it, and I was perplexed at why she let it bother her so much. I figured my innocence and my commitment to her should be enough. Alas, I was wrong.

Shortly after we got married in her father's compound in Opokuma, near Yenagoa and then in church, she started withdrawing from people. Trust became her staple word. "I don't trust all these girls," she would say, eyes scanning the room like a hawk, "they like to go for married men."

By this time she had left the choir but I was still playing the piano and the drums and now, teaching group vocal lessons because Tariela had insisted she did not want me alone with any woman. My attempts to explain that we were in open space in church was only met with, "it does not matter, what will people say?" She would ask determinedly.

When I mentioned my integrity, she would concede with, "I trust you babes, it is the thirsty women I don't trust." Like slowly ebbing erosion, my obedience to higher demands, only fuelled her suspicion.

The next request was for us to start attending the Anglican Church downtown at Amarata, downtown Yenagoa, because there were more married people there who could mentor us. I knew why she wanted it. The average age there was over fifty, no one there could be looking at her man.

I refused on principle. How could we change a church for a frivolous reason like that? She threatened and cried that I don't understand. I explained and try to allay her fears. The inevitable day came when I was helping my pastor's wife record and produce her single in church. I was there with another member of staff, a male, as well as her personal assistant.

My project was on hold, at that time. I was not expected to come on site. Although I would go to work, there was not much happening. This means that I could leave at any time. Tariela, who should be getting out of work by 5pm, was in the church by 3pm. She walked in shouting and cussing "Useless woman! You want to sleep with my husband abi? I've caught you today."

I absolutely believed she had gone mental I rushed out of the booth to hold her because she was lunging at the stupefied clergy woman who was at least a decade, older than I was.

"Tariela now... we are recording. What is the matter? Why are you acting like this?" I tried to reason with her.

"Ehn, *abeg abeg abeg,* that's what they always say, I don't trust any of you. I can see that you're sleeping with her. I traced you on your iPhone. Were you not supposed to be at work? Why are you here, tell me, If you are not doing mago-mago? I have caught you today!"

Unhinged was the word and I left the church that day knowing I could not be back. Maybe that was Tariela's intention. If it was, she had won. I could not bear the embarrassment. After a rough week she started apologising. With the same excuses of women being thirsty and lusting after other people's husbands.

We started attending the Anglican Church she wanted. I loved the classical music there as well. It reminded me of my secondary school days and I was eager to get engaged with the musicians there. Tariela had an immediate response to that, "Halim, that's always where the home-destroyers are... these days, they don't stand on the road o. They go to church where you will not suspect that they ensnare you. I will not let you expose yourself to the devil, my husband pa si sei." she pleaded, "let us worship God from the pews here."

At times like these, I would stop listening and tune her out. I was beginning to consider it almost like a mental illness. My wife Tariela had issues, and did I want to make my marriage work? Yes. However, this was beginning to chip away at my freedom in the grasp of this marriage. It was choking.

It rose to the point where my friends started calling to say that Tariela had been calling to check on me and to investigate all of my whereabouts. She would accuse them of lying to cover up for me. These were upstanding men. She had also been reaching out to my secretary to keep tabs on me. Tariela had become obsessive with this self-assigned task.

It took me a while to realise that this was not a phase she would likely grow out of. It became clear when we moved to Abuja, some 700km away. My project had concluded, and the transfer she requested was granted. I saw it as a fresh start. I was happy, she was happy. We could focus on our family. And this was what she always wanted, to move out of that city with thirsty girls.

I let her pick the church, and we settled into our new community. I knew by this time female friends were essentially forbidden, and my music had been all but quashed. Anywhere girls were, basically, I could not be.

Not many things impede trust as much as control. The more she meddled and investigated me, the more she set limits on my activities by her tantrums, the more I felt constrained and controlled. But looking at her, it was hard to see. There she was, unduly concerned and worried. Outwardly, she was not the picture of a controlling person. And I, who had not done anything wrong, would have to plead my case, every day, and declare my innocence. It was as unfair as if I had been placed in handcuffs for a crime that had not even been committed.

I snuck out of that bathroom quietly, faster than I typically would have. Startled, she gasped and hastily dropped the phone. She forced a laugh that sounded sharp and embarrassed.

"Why, Tariela, why...?" I asked, broken.
"What is it? I was just looking at something. Can't I check your phone again?" she defended.
"I can't do this anymore. We need to talk to someone." I was done.

I think she thought I was joking because that evening when I gave her a list of three marriage counsellors: two men and a middle-aged woman from church, she tried to make light of it,

"I mean, it's not that serious now."
"I know you don't think it is Tariela, but I am no longer free under the shadow of your suspicion, it's affecting our marriage. And we can't continue like this." I continued,
"Last month you called my Executive Director at work, because you thought I was using it to hide my mistress' name, my friends or family can't come close because you are suspicious of everybody".

She started coming on to bed, stroking my arm and mumbling, "Oya sorry now". I felt myself getting weaker, but I was not done. I stood up from the chair, "Let me finish please, Tariela. I apologise for my part in this. I have been enabling you, and should have let you know from the get-go, how this has impacted me and how it is not even healthy for you to continue this way."

With finality I continued, "I can't force you. But if we don't go figure out what all these are about then we cannot continue like this."

I gave her a week to think through. My ultimatum was that if I did not hear back with her selection, as much as I hated it, I would have to escalate it to my family and hers to begin talks to discuss the dissolution of the marriage. Overkill, I hear you say, not if you lived with Tariela. The sleuth, with whom every question was an interrogation and every comment suggestive. My every action was suspect, and her every move was strategy of some sort to ward off imaginary people. Done, I was. Emphatically yes.

I moved out the week after, true to my words. Her pleas came through on several voice notes and texts. I responded to them with, "I can meet you at the counsellor's office, but not anywhere else". I changed my phone because I knew she could track me. Don't ask me how, Tariela always finds a way.

She chose the woman. A sagely Christian who was a board certified, internationally trained marriage counsellor and psychologist. After several sessions, Tariela began to share the strongholds that plagued her. Her dad cheated on her mum repeatedly, but her mum was in oblivion, or chose not to see.

Tariela had caught her dad red-handed, a couple of times, in the house with women when her mum was away, and at his office. She never did tell her mum because she did not want to cause her pain. Her dad knew that she had become complicit when she did not tell. He would come pick her from school with a strange woman in his car and trusted that she would not breathe a word. It was so excruciating; she knew she did not want her mum to feel the pain. She was going to shield her from it.

Somewhere, she had come to believe all men lie and cheat, even the good ones. They had to be stopped before they succumbed to the inevitable. A woman must not leave her man unchecked. It was eye opening for me, and I felt more empathy. I thought she was just stressing me out. I did not know she was experiencing deep emotional guilt, fear and hurt.

We still see the therapist once a month, but she has given us the tools that are helping us keep our marriage healthier now. I have joined a band, an all-male one, that ministers at churches. She does not badger me incessantly, anymore; we are learning to trust again.

THE WIZENED EXAMPLE

I watched the grey-haired couple from my vantage perch on the broken concrete fence. They had walked out again religiously at 6pm same as the last couple of years since my aunt moved to the area. I had not first noticed them till I started to pay attention, a few months later. They would addle out, one foot closely behind the other. Her hand would clutch her walking stick and he would walk behind her slightly with his hand on her shoulder. I don't know now if he was egging her on with support, or he was leaning on her for sturdiness. Whichever way, there was always some contact between them. Then they would reach the wicker double chair on the front porch and, almost in synchrony, lower themselves on to the chair. I noticed sometimes they would chat animatedly with gesticulations and, at other times, they would sit quietly with their eyes gazing outwards, but still together. Sometimes, smiling and other times not. I wondered why I did not think they were angry. I guess it was the peace that their union exuded. What was that feeling? Contentment? I almost did not want to break the reverie of their harmony.

But, of course, they saw me and waved.

"Amina, how are you? Welcome back from school," Mr. Horsfall greeted wearing a confused look on his handsomely aged face. "But isn't it too soon to be back now?" He was pointing to me, but his eyes would turn towards her, as though expecting the response from her.

"Sir, it's ASUU strike o..." I answered as I walked towards their house, a few yards away, to greet them. I was referring to the Academic Staff Union of Universities. I continued, "The lecturers don't want us to graduate."

"Don't worry." they started almost simultaneously, looking at me, and Mrs. Horsfall added, "You will graduate," just as her husband chimed in, in finality, "In Jesus name."

As she tried to stand up so her hand could touch me as she began her routine blessing, he reached to help her and I ran the next couple of yards, shouting "Don't worry, don't worry, Ma." When I got to her, I fell to my knees as the Yorubas customarily kneel to elders... a sign of respect.

I could hear my grandma's voice from when I was five.

You should never see the top of a grey head. Ah, do you want to bring curses on your head? When they are standing up, you should lower your head. When they're sitting, you should be kneeling.

"Abi, you don't have respect?" She would ask sternly.
I'd respond intrigued, "But what if they are kneeling down?"
"Ah, *o ti ku niyen o*. Then you better dobale. Be lying down quick, quick."
As I would laugh, she would lunge at me, half seriously.
As I knelt to greet my wizened neighbours, her fleeting memory brought back nostalgic memories and a tear dropped.
"Ah, don't cry, it will be okay," Mrs Horsfall said.

I realized that they thought my sadness was from not being in school, but I did not bother them with further details. They placed their aged hands on my back and started the prayer -greetings that elders habitually performed on demand, in any setting.

"It will be well with you, my child. As you went to school, so will you graduate," said Mr Horsfall. Her hands shook a little and she paused then continued, "You and your colleagues will find favor in the government's sight."
"And you will return in no time." Mr. Horsfall added.
"Ah, just the prayer we always offer for our son in America." Mrs Horsfall said.

It all seemed like a dance of words, in which they had mastered their parts and finished each other's sentences smoothly.

After this lyrical prayer with me bobbing my head murmuring Amens, she added, "And when you finish, a good man like Daddy will be waiting to marry you."

I chuckled and made to get up as Mr. Horsfall interjected, "Ah, Mommy allow her to graduate first now." laughing along with me.

"It's never too early, you know." she said with a glint in her eyes.
"Neither is it ever too late," he added, tickling her chin, "my *Oyoyo* Baby. "They burst out laughing as they turned to look at each other.

I blushed and walked towards the beautiful porch garden with the tropical array of ixora and hibiscus plants. The sunflower was blooming, and the Ivy was almost halfway up the house now. I remembered when it was a third way up. As I slipped away down the stairs of the porch following the curve of the ixora hedge, I could hear them still talking, but could not make out the words. My departure had not quite registered with them.

Halfway to my house and still within earshot, I called out "Good night, Sir and Ma."

"Ehen, good night, my daughter." I heard back.

Shortly after, I left my aunt's to go stay with my grandma in the village. She was recovering from a fall, and I went to nurse her back to health. It was hard to see how frail she had become: the woman who raised me, with a strong hand after her only child, my mom had died in childbirth, was aging. And it was a humbling sight to see how the illness had tamed her.

Mama was one of four wives that my grandfather had married. He died shortly after she had her first baby at 19, two years into their marriage. She never remarried. So, I had little example of a monogamous loving relationship in our still traditional and quaint village of Owena.

Growing up, my grandma constantly warned me of boys in the community. If she had stopped there, I could have borne it. But no, she would also personally warn them to stay away from me. I stood no chance of having a boyfriend. Thankfully, I was only interested in Maths and Physics, all as abstract as the world beyond Owena, and the nearby market town, Ilesha, where we went to sell produce.

So, before I received a scholarship to Nigeria's premier University of Ibadan, I had never been out of my local government area. Grandma reached out to the community chief who was happy to support his diligent "daughter" with the address of one of the illustrious daughters of Owena. Mrs Lara Osho, deputy registrar and lecturer at the University of Ibadan. She lived on the outskirts of the university in a suburb called Bodija. That was where I was living when I met Mr. And Mrs. Horsfall.

After grandma recuperated to that level of wellness where it did not seem like she was at death's door, I went back to school and quickly got busy finishing up my medical degree with its numerous internships, so that I did not visit Auntie Lara for over a year, going straight from school to Owena to check on Grandma.

Of course, this left little time to spare on dating. I noticed grandma had started prodding me with *"oko e nko"*. I would always digress, asking her if she still wanted me to be a doctor. Truth be told, I did not quite see marriage in my future. What would it look or feel like to live with a boy? No, a man: for the rest of my life. I fought hard trying to picture it till I noticed my hands were pressed against my temple, as if to squeeze a thought out. I laughed out loud when I realized the ridiculousness.

Then, my thoughts strayed to Mr and Mrs Horsfall, the lovely couple who lived opposite my aunt. The thought made me smile and I made a mental note to see them that weekend, as I turned out my bedside lamp to sleep.

It was some months later when I went to stay at Aunty Lara's in Bodija. I decided to check on the Horsfalls.

It was 6:15pm. And I was expecting them to be on their usual spots on the front porch. The last time I was there, Mr Horsfall was in a wheelchair, from a debilitating disease he had, while Mrs Horsfall was now using a walker, but they still made it outside. There was a caregiver who would help them with meals and moving around. Had they gone for a check-up? I mused as I rapped warmly on the front door and greeted *"E kaale,* Sir o... *Se daadaa,* Ma."

A strange face peered through the window before opening the door. As the door swung open, I saw the quizzical smile on his interesting dark chocolate face with a full head of thick curls.

I said, "Who are you?" and he was asking the same question.I smiled and pointed across to Mrs Osho's house.
"Oh," he beamed, the moustache framing a full pink-lipped smile. "Come in."
It was my turn to be curious.
"Mommy and Daddy mentioned you," he said, making way for me to get into the living room.
"Oh, you are the son in America," I surmised. Then it dawned on me. "Did they travel?"

His face fell and the glint in his eyes was replaced by wistful emotion and he dropped the news.

"They both passed within one week of each other three weeks ago," he said. "Mommy had an aneurysm and daddy had diabetes, or maybe he just wanted to be with mummy." He smiled sadly. "That's how they always were... stubbornly inseparable from even before I was born."

I stood there, mouth agape in disbelief, as he continued.

"They told me they could not have children, for the first 11 years of their marriage, so they learned to take care of each other, and enjoy each other's company, before I came along". I was still standing there, frozen, as he paced around. Speaking as if to an audience, or to no one, he said in a subdued tone, "My Dad would tell me it was not always like that. He would say how my Mom cried endlessly, and how he resented not having a child, till they were on the brink of separation. Then they decided to give their marriage one last shot. It took another four years for them to have me, but by this time they were so in love that they were resolved to enjoy their marriage regardless."

He noticed I was reaching to lean on the wall as he quickly reached out a hand to support me and led me to a chair. "Are you okay? Sorry I've been talking the whole time." I nodded and shook my head.

"Well, you must have been close to them because they left a package for you." He handed me something heavy, wrapped in a cloth. "Would you like to open it?"

As I unveiled it, I saw it was a frame. The same one I had admired the few times I had been in there. And the one they had shown me, the one time I had asked the secret to their marriage. On it was inscribed,
I am responsible for my happiness.
You are responsible for your happiness.
That's why we're so happy together.

I smiled through my tears, and he quickly grabbed some tissue and asked again, “Are you okay?” As I wiped my eyes, he said, “You will be okay,” and we both ended, “in Jesus name.” I smiled through my tears and looked at my hands in his and both our hands on the frame.

Today, he is my husband of six years and we lead a marriage ministry in our church in Mount Pleasant, Michigan. Mr and Mrs Horsfall, my in-laws of blessed memory left journals that we have repurposed for courses and teachings. When we are not at our busy medical practice in Saginaw, we are having a fun time with our two boisterous boys away, every month at our cabin at the lake. Or sometimes, it’s just Dare and me on the front porch, lounging in our hammock or sitting in the rocking wicker chairs, with the boys away at sleepover at our friends.

(WIFE) HUSBAND TRAINING

What kind of man cannot hold his own home? Any man who cannot control his wife is worse than an infidel. His mind pondered, even as he misquoted the scripture. He knew what to do. He was raised to be a man.

"A real man is not subject to his emotions." his soccer coach in secondary school would always say. So, regardless of what he felt, he put his feelings in a box and locked them away, affirming his resolve with a decisive action, the kind of action he was about to take on his wife of five years.

Yes, he loved her and would give his life for her in a heartbeat, but she started growing wings recently; and those wings needed to be clipped.

"In a home, there is only one head," his dad often told him. "Anything with two heads is a monster." Francis, himself, had also repeated this to several of his friends in their bid to quash the rebellion and gain authority in their homes. He thought about it in military terms because, to him, it was not much different than mutiny; this flagrant subversion by women, *who now think they are equal to men. Arrant nonsense! If it is easy, they should go and work and bring money to the house now.*

His own wife, Simi, worked and earned good money. Although, he thought: *Is that not because I allow her to work? She does not even know she is playing with fire. I will just ban her from that work. Women never know their place: you give them an inch and they take a mile. That is why you must subjugate them, show them who is the boss, and that you are not afraid to act decisively and swiftly as the man that you are. That is why the way you start out in marriage is so important. A man must lay down the gauntlet and draw the line from the beginning.*

“Don’t smile anyhow, in your house,” he often coached his friends. “Marriage is not the same as dating and familiarity breeds contempt. If you smile anyhow now, tomorrow somebody will insult you. Why would you bring that upon yourself?”

He remembered the long marriage lectures that he often gave to his friends. He had a blueprint for schooling them so they could take charge in their homes.

“It’s best to make yourself scarce so that when they see you, they will value you. Always lock your phone to discourage her from trying to pry, not that you have anything to hide but for the principle that you do not answer to her. Hang out with the boys till midnight. She will probably start texting you from nine o’clock in the night, asking when you will be home. Just send her a brief reply: *‘Soon.’*

“If she pesters you too much, turn off your phone. You are not a child, and any woman who thinks she can dictate her husband’s itinerary is a controlling spirit that must be stopped. If she is the stubborn kind, she will start shouting when you get home."

"First, warn her. If she won't stop, then get back in your car and drive away. Sleep in a hotel and turn off your phone. When you wake up by ten o'clock in the morning, you will see about ten missed calls and another fifteen text messages. Humility would have visited her by then, and the apologies would start pouring in. Don't reply. Have breakfast there, check out at eleven o'clock in the morning and go home."

"She will be waiting for you with another meal. Don't eat immediately. Consider her remorse before you call her later to formally forgive her. Don't forget to take what you are due in bed; she would be more than willing. Who wants to lose their husband to Lagos girls? If she is the type that wants to use sex to punish you, you must deal with her mercilessly. Even when she wants you, tell her she needs to start losing the baby weight that is long overdue or tell her anything to put her in her place."

"Sleep on the couch downstairs for no reason. Most of all hold yourself, don't worry; it's only for a short while. And if you pass the exam, she won't try that nonsense again. Anytime you even raise your own eyebrows, na she go dey rush you."

"When you will know you have trained her very well is when you will hear her advising other women on the lessons you taught her the hard way. For example, you will her saying, 'Don't check your husband's phone' or 'You have to forgive and let go, no matter the offence, even infidelity.' Her advice would be 'After all, you should be grateful that you are the official Mrs.'"

"Ndi Nwanyi, we sabi dem finish. Mumu button for where? Taah! Who born dem?", he would end with a boast, "Me, Francis? Dem never born the woman wey wan carry me see road. I am a full-blooded man. I will not tolerate it."

That is why Francis did not quite understand the changes in his home. Simi had changed from the impressionable good girl he married just after they graduated from their master's degree programmes in the United Kingdom. According to his timeless formula, he got her around the age when a woman would want to be engaged and start her career, the point when any delay could lead to desperation.

Going by his formula, she was almost over educated and over age for the typical guy, especially as she did not have a boyfriend when they met. Then, it was a plus that she was from a good family who had never had a scandal; and he was sure that she would not want to be the one to bring shame to their spotless reputation. He had taken her through all the phases of the "training". She has borne the two children he told her he wanted, two boys. As an Odogwu, he is well represented.

The misbehaviour started with a book she read, Simi was an avid reader, and he had supported the habit because no one wants a *waka-jugbe* wife that will follow all those other women who seek to spoil the good ones. Yes, Simi had always been a good wife, but of course, he had never told her that because women have a way of letting these things get to their heads. So, he appreciated her with brief nods and half smiles when she served his food. Sometimes, he deliberately did not comment on how the food tasted because he did not want to spoil all his hard work of training.

But there was something about the book she received at the Women's Bible Study from one of the pastors that came from America. Of course, he liked that she attended church. He did sometimes too, but he would never be one of those fathers standing at Children's Church after service, waiting for their children. What happened to their mothers? Un-trained! That is what they are. He always wished he could teach these fathers so they would be men of their own homes.

When Simi mentioned that the Bible study women started a book club, he had simply nodded because his words were few. By now, Simi has learned than to ask for his opinions and feelings. All she asked for was permission because there were dire consequences for going against his wish.

Then, he noticed her strange behaviour since she started attending the book club. Basically, she was *trying* him. He could not place his fingers on it just yet, but he knew. He could see it in her eyes; a certainty that felt challenging to him. She now walked and talked with confidence, like a British royalty. *Was she daring me? She should not try herself o. She knows I will handle her swiftly,* he thought

So far, she had not come out plainly, but there was something about how she hummed around the house and carried on with that assuredness; and he now had to watch her closely. He returned from hanging out with the boys the other day, and was surprised that she was awake because she knew better now than to wait up for him. That is, unless he returned and woke her up to prepare a meal for him if he was hungry. But he went ahead to casually inquire, and she said she was working on a book.

"She wants to be an author!" Francis thought as he burst out laughing. Who does she think she is? *Author my foot!* To remind her of her place, he asked for her to serve his food and

almost immediately, she pointed at the dining room saying, "Dinner is served. It's on the table." *The nerve of her!*
As she sat back down to resume her writing, he asked her to go warm the cold food.
"I just did before you came in." Then, she had the gall to add, "Bon Appetit!"

Francis felt so incensed that he wanted to hit her.

But that was one rule to never flout, according to his training sessions to the guys; *never get physical with your wife. Her parents or even the police may get involved, and that would put you in a bad light. This is why you should train her from a place of strategy; it was so that even her family would love you. Everyone knows a woman is supposed to behave, and nobody wants their daughter to go and disgrace them in her husband's house.*

So, over the next couple of days, he decided to open his goodie bag of punishments; no eating, silent treatment, and absence for hours at a time. That, he was sure, would bring her crawling to beg and ask what she did wrong. Then, he could quell this nascent rebellion because this is how disloyalty creeps up when men do not pay attention.

A week had passed, and she had not come begging or crying for him to eat her food or touch her. She was holding her head even higher, if it were possible, and singing songs and having the nerve to be happy. Even during morning devotion with the kids, which of course he left for her to organize, she was thanking God for blessing her with joy, peace, love and laughter! *Laughter ke? Is she laughing at me?*

No, Francis could take no more, so he summoned her upstairs, but Simi did not scurry up as usual.

"I'm coming." she called out to say, before gracefully climbing up the stairs.

He knew this because he had heard her steps, like in a cadence, measured and deliberate.

"This nonsense will not happen in my home!" Francis decreed as soon as Simi walked in.
"What are you talking about?" She asked, sweetly. "Tell me, Francis, so I can help you."
"Simi, you help me?" Francis was incredulous at this point. "When did that rubbish start that a small rat like you wants to help me?"
Her smile disappeared, and he saw a firm face that he had never seen before.
"Francis, please don't call me names. I am here to answer you.

Talk to me like a person, please."
"I will talk to you however the bloody hell I please! You are a stupid girl without a brain. I'm talking, and you have the guts to open your mouth. Since when, Simi?"
"Since I realised, I am a person of value and deserving of love and respect." She said calmly.

As he opened his mouth to put her squarely in her place, she raised her hand and said,

"Francis, you called me and I'm here to listen. Please, talk to me. But if you call me names or insult me, I will not be here to listen to it."
"How dare you Simi?" Francis asked, foaming at the mouth. "You dare disrespect me like this. How dare you?"
"You are raising your voice at me, Francis."

This calm Simi angered him as much as it scared him, and the expletives started pouring out of his mouth. After about ten seconds, Simi looked at him, dead set in my eyes and turned on her heels to leave the room.
"You better turn back now... else you will regret your life!" he called after her, just as their son came up the stairs and said, "Daddy, why are you shouting?"

"Let me know when you are ready to talk." Simi said as she walked away, holding their son's hands.

Francis almost broke his fists as he slammed them into the concrete walls; he was shaken to the core, but he managed to find his keys and stormed out of the house. He drove to the next street and pulled up at the corner and tried to control his shaking body, but he could not recognise this feeling coursing through him. It was neither anger nor rage; it was not sadness; but it was consuming. Why did it make me want to hide? Then, he realised with a flush that it was shame, and it was coming in waves.

Francis had never lost the battle, and he always prided himself in how he had held it all together these five years. His perfectly trained wife was misbehaving, and his tailored life was unravelling before his eyes. Francis did not know what to do, but for the first time in years, he cried. He cried for the man he had become. The weight of his masculinity was crushing, and he could hear the expectations that society had of him. He had done everything right. How on earth was this happening to him? He was not sure where he failed, but he had to get this right.

He picked up his phone and called his uncle to tell him all that had transpired. He wanted to know how to navigate this from an expert. Uncle Tunde's wife, Aunty Mary was very well behaved, courteous, and respectful. And there were no problems in their house.

After listening to Francis' complaints, his burst into laughter.

"Francis, your *mumu* don ripe o. How could you do that?"

"Uncle, wasn't this what you taught me?" Francis asked, perplexed.

"But that's just boys' talk. That's locker room talk. We stop there and go home, and we behave ourselves. Look, you think you want to train your wife but she's the one training you here. We never push them to this place where they have to respond. You have pushed her to the wall, and a woman scorned... well you know what they say. So you better go back and make this right, because even me, I wouldn't try that."

"Uncle, what do you mean?" Francis asked, petulant. "You always put Aunty Mary in her place. She won't try this rubbish with you—"
"And I will not try this rubbish with her because I know that I can push her too far. So, you go back and make this right. At the end of the day, Francis, there are two of you in that

marriage. Even though you are a husband, she's a human being, too. Better go and work your marriage. If you ruin this, I will not follow you to beg her family o."

After the call, Francis sat in his car, wondering how and where to begin. What would his friends think, especially the ones he had coached over time? Where was he to begin from? What would happen when he apologises to Simi and makes things right like his uncle had advised? Wouldn't she start to be the one oppressing him? Was it possible to be partners in a marriage?

Why did it matter so much to him that Simi remained his doormat? Had he not cheered and praised women who were blazing trails? What did their husbands do differently? He knew, without a doubt, that he loved his wife and that he had some learning to do if he still wanted his marriage. He kick started the car, which felt like a ton, made a U-turn and started on his way back home.

When he got home, he heard her with the kids upstairs. As he stood to collect himself before going to have this talk of a lifetime, his eyes caught the red book on the table, opened in the middle, facing downwards beside the journal she had been taking notes in. The name of the book: Boundaries: When to Say Yes, How to Say No to Take Control of Your Life by Henry Cloud and John Townsend.

MS. MEDDLESOME

When she was about to start judging, you could tell from her face. It was in the way her mouth shifted upwards, how her nose twisted slightly. Then her eyes would follow suit, widening and narrowing in exaggeration. That's how I knew that judgment was about to start. And I would brace myself internally in a futile attempt to be ready for the scathing words to follow.

And flow they did. In the feisty quickness of tongue that a Bendel girl could unleash on a deserving person. Mummy grew up in her beloved Warri, a city where street smarts and feistiness were a cultural showcase. Even little kids grow up with wit and grit. That was the substance she was made of.

When her tone was not cutting, they were nuanced: hinting at inadequacies, or suggesting better ways of being, for things out of my control. Like when I was trying to save for my ticket to the US. We both went to the market and were buying hair products at the Beauty Supply store. She was admiring some wigs and even tried one on. The issue started when she casually asked me to buy it for her. It was pricey, and I had already paid for the hair products. When I tried to explain that I could not, she responded,

"Is it not your mates who are buying it?"

Of course, my hesitant explanations of the status quo only escalated things as she doubled down, "This kind of man you want to marry that cannot even buy your ticket complete... that one sef na husband?" Then she rolled her eyes and stood up in that condescending manner as she finished, "Abeg I no wan hear anything wey go make me vex, nonsense".

That was my mom, not one to miss an opportunity to share her opinion or impose her will.

That was four years ago, and Odafe and I are now living, working and making a home in Houston, Texas in the United States. My mom had just arrived from the airport to see my new-born baby who arrived five weeks before I was due back at work, six weeks postpartum, in no less a place than America, the self-proclaimed greatest country on Earth.

Most other countries mandated at least a twelve-week maternity leave, others as much as six months to a year. And very well so, because birthing a baby takes its toll in every way, then add on the responsibility providing care to a new-born. In Nigeria, I would have a barrage of family: grandmas, aunties and nannies to help care for the baby and the new mum. I had no such luxuries here.

As it stood, I was barely healed physically. My body was sore in tissue and muscles I never even knew existed in my body. My mental health was a question my doctor asked me at every Baby Wellness visit.

Am I well?
Have I been taking care of myself?
Do I have help?

Yes, No and No.

First, wellness was not a choice. It was what I had to be for my new-born baby whose sustenance I had become. So yes, I am well, that is, I take care of my baby. No, I have not been taking time for myself. Where would I find it? Odafe had resumed work after his three-day paternity leave. He was out of vacation days now because he had been nursing me since I had been on bedrest the last month of my pregnancy. I knew how badly he wanted to be there for our baby boy, Obaro and me. That is why I never complained.

I also knew he had to have a good night's rest for his tasking job as Production Manager at his manufacturing plant. So, I tried not to bother him much during the night. But he would wake up at 4am and be with baby till he had to leave at 6.30am. He would gently kiss me to say he was leaving and return the baby monitor to my bedside. As soon as the door shut behind him, I would cry my first tears for the day, in what was becoming a habit. I don't know if I cried out of despair, as much as loneliness when he left.

I mean, I was not lonely because I had my beautiful baby with me. But I was alone, all by myself with him. And I was everything for him. His milk jug, diaper changer, his body rocker, and his Man or *Woman Friday*. I have never been that much to anybody in my life, especially as the last born of six children. Born five years after my immediate elder brother.

Growing up, every home I ever saw a baby in, had a ton of people waiting hands and foot on Mum and Baby. So, no, I did not have any help. But I was mighty glad my mother was arriving soon, when we believed we needed her the most, then I would have to return to work so she could stay the five months before her visa with visiting term of six months expired.

Under normal circumstances, I would have been apprehensive about mom's visit because we all knew how "engaged" she could get with sharing her opinion and offering suggestions. That was more like forcing suggestions, which started out with seemingly good intentions, but they always morphed into Hobson's choices, my way or the highway.

I managed a chuckle; things would be different now. I am married and have my own home now. A full-fledged adult with a family. I was getting to make my own rules in my home. With Obaro and our growing family, I felt the burst of joy again as the whiff of the baby powder I was dousing him in, wafted across my face. He was a chubby and angel-faced baby with skin the color of caramel.

These moments overshadowed any other doubts or sadness, I could conceive and may have experienced through the day. For now, I was fulfilled with a heart bursting with love and gratitude.

I picked mum up from the George Bush intercontinental airport in Houston that afternoon. She went straight for Obaro, cuddling and squeezing and kissing him. She was singing as well. It was a song Grandma would sing to us when we were younger. I had expected some more greetings and concern for me. But I figured she was more excited about the newborn. So, I let it go.

I packed her luggage into the trunk and wanted to borrow from her reluctant hands, Obaro to place him in his car seat. She started with, “Let me carry him on my laps now.”

“Don’t worry, latest Grandma, you don’t have to. Rest, you hear? Till we get home...”

“How can I rest when my grandson is alone by himself. I came here to carry him. Allow me jare.” she said, getting flustered. By now the traffic warden had started waving us on. I realized she was not going to budge, so I had to let her know, "Mommy, police will hold us o. It's against the law for baby to ride in your arms." I reached for him more firmly, strapped him in and shut the door.

She complained all the way back to the house and railed against all these modern-day parents and how we treated our children like bastards. That had left an acerbic taste in my mouth. But I did not want to ruin the day. So I bit my tongue and let it go.

That night with Odafe and I fast asleep in our bedroom, adjacent to the baby room, we heard a loud rap on the door. It was so loud I thought it was police raid from my half sleepiness. I jumped up only to see my mum in my room. She had not only come in, she turned on the light and in her hands was Obaro sleeping peacefully as she rocked him on her shoulder. Mom had gone to sleep early jetlag from her trip, having travelled thousands of miles and across hours of time zones.

Through my momentary shock, I saw she was shouting at this point, "How can you leave this baby to sleep by himself in another room? While you people are here enjoying yourselves? What kind of nonsense is this? Isioma, is this how I brought you up?"

"Mommy, what are you... Who are you...?" I stuttered. I had hardly slept an hour from breastfeeding the baby and I was still groggy. Behind me, Odafe sprang up too, scanning the room. Eyes darting, checking for the threat, asking

"What happened? What's happening, Mommy?"

My eyes caught the clock, it was 2:30am. Her aim achieved, my mum started walking out, still muttering, "I never seen this type of thing. A new-born's mother will leave her baby and go and sleep."

I urged my husband back to bed, "You need to sleep, Baby. It's okay. She just wanted me to feed him." I lied to allay his concern. I followed her out into the living room of our small three-bedroom apartment.

"But Mommy, it's okay for him to sleep there."

She hushed me, "Shut up your mouth there. If that was what I did with you, will you be alive today? It's not because you have come to Obodo Oyibo that you will be a wicked somebody. If I did not go into that room now, what would have happened to this baby, ehn?"

All the noise and movement woke Obaro. And he gave a wail, that nasally newborn cry that snuffs out any sleep.

"Sorry, mommy" I begrudged, still sore and angry. "Was he crying?"
She shook her head casually, "No. I just went to pee and saw him there all by himself."
I could not believe it. She had picked a perfectly sleeping, well-fed and dry diaper baby, up from his bed.

I could not handle the thought. For the next couple of days, I slept in the baby nursery to avoid the side eyes and talk. Even though I was seething from that night. I rationalized it. She was just an old-school grandma who cares for her grandson. Odafe asked me to leave the baby in the nursery like we had planned originally, saying that I needed the rest and that we were "spoiling" the baby. All the parenting books we had diligently studied said to establish a routine early and stick to it so the baby gets used to it so I understood his concern. I explained to him that this wasn't going to be forever. "When Mommy goes, I will return. Let's not ruffle any feathers now." He did not understand why I would let her have such sway. How could he understand? He was not there when my dad passed, and my mom had to raise us all by herself. She did a fine job of making sure we never lacked, dedicating her life to her children. Even when suitors came, she would not consider remarrying even though she was just thirty-seven.

When he passed, she got even more involved in our lives, knew our teachers and handpicked our friends. With a non-smiley face, when an undesirable acquaintance would visit, she could eliminate a friend just like that with her words and attitude. She, including courses of study in the university, handpicked all our schools.

I had already shamed her by not marrying a wealthy Nigerian doctor who lived in the Middle East that had worshipped her. I was determined not to incur her anger during this trip. The subtle snide comments continued about many different things. The way I looked, what baby wore, food we ate, everything.

Another thing she came up with was the untidy mess of my room. My room was not dirty, I just had clothes spewed all over the place. That was the least of my concerns right now. But what did it matter, it was my room.

"Mommy, don't worry, we are okay. Leave it like that. We know where everything is."
She said, "You don't know jare. You're a married woman so behave like one. See how everywhere is scattered."

Then she would say, "I give you till tomorrow to do something."

She said it again the other day, it was so ridiculous and I laughed it off. So, when Odafe called me at work the next day, I was not expecting it, "Your mom is in our drawers, folding and rearranging everything... even my condoms!"

"What?" I felt the chill in my bones.

He told me all his pleas for her to stop had fallen on deaf ears. And how she had kept right on talking and going, "This is how things are supposed to be arranged. You children are too scattered. Please behave like adults."

The last straw was when Odafe told me she had referred to the condom saying, "Won't you allow my daughter to heal? Someone who just had a baby. Men are insatiable o."

When I returned, I found true to his story: Odafe's previously dirty underwear boxers all washed and folded neatly in the shower while the said condoms conspicuously placed on our bedroom and desk. I knew it was time to have the conversation I had been dreading.

I texted Odafe, who had felt sufficiently embarrassed enough to leave the house, and I asked him not to return for another couple of hours. I could not tell what specifically to expect from the talk. But I knew it was long overdue. It would not be pretty. Somewhere in my mum's mind, all her children were still kids who needed taking care of and who needed her to keep mothering.

This had somehow deteriorated into a pseudo control that had me lying and dodging issues because her emotions were like eggshells that I had to tiptoe around. Last week, I had confided in my Auntie Awele, mom's younger sister. Just as feisty, but more free-spirited and open-minded. My mother hated her guts; because she would not live like her wiser, elder sister had planned for her.

Auntie had laughed and said, "You know your mom. She will not stop unless you stand up to her." So, with sweaty palms, and a shaky voice, I stepped up to her that evening in the living room, where she sat in the recliner, rocking my baby, her first grandson for whom she had already grown a bond.

She had her snacks within arm's reach on the stool, and the drink. I knew a lot depended on this moment. I could not do five more months of this. And my emotions were already raw and on edge to the point that my doctor had been more concerned about me than the baby.

That week when I went to get the baby vaccinated, one thing Dr Evans asked me to do was not just asked for help, but to ask for the kind of help that I needed. She also told me to set boundaries and not let anyone else put pressure on me.

"Mummy, please can I talk with you?" I sat down on the small stool beside her seat as she gently swung back and forth. "Please, I want to ask you, to please respect our boundaries." I got a sharp look from her and I diverted from her piercing eyes and continued quickly for fear I would not get it all out. "Meaning what now?" she started, eyes narrowing.

"It's just the way you talk to Odafe and I," I continued shakily without trying to catch my breath so I could say everything as quickly as possible, "How you don't respect our spaces. Like our room..."

She cut in, "Ehn Isioma, if you want to insult me, just go ahead... I don't blame you. It's because I am in your house, doing Omugwo. But that does not give you the right to disrespect me. You hear? Let that rubbish stop now!"

I tried to cajole her, holding her hand. "You see what I was saying, Mommy, you are not letting me speak freely to you. Please hear me out. Odafe too did not like how you spoke to him."

She had heard enough. With all the self-righteousness she could muster, she threw the biggest tantrum and started with all she had done to make me who I am in this life. After all the sacrifice, see how I was treating her. How all she ever had; she gave to us. And now, no one respected her. And how everyone felt they had the right to talk to her anyhow.

I do not know how I got the fortitude to remain seated and or unmoved. I fought every urge to go down on my knees and appease her in that moment. After all, I would live. I would live to fight another day.

But I heard Aunty Awele's voice again, "Whenever you decide to talk to her. Whatever she says, don't back down or else the cycle will continue over again."

I remembered Dr. Evans saying, "Be sincere. Talk to someone. Ask for help."

And I remained resolute. She summarily handed me the baby and began crying. I just listened to her in silence, my hands hugging my chest tightly as though I was the one crying and in need of comforting.

Then I said, "I know you love me, Mummy. But please, I don't want to hide from you. Help me by letting me be myself, and leave Odafe and I be. All the food you see in the freezer. I did not even cook them. But I repacked everything in our bowls after reheating in our pots. Just so you could believe I cooked them by myself. Isn't it ridiculous that I think I should do that to stop you from shouting again?"

The words were pouring hot from my deep place of hurt, as I continued, unable to stop myself.

"Every time you refer to my breast milk supply as too small and compare it with when you took care of us, I would go to the car and cry because I felt like the worst mother. I could never be you."

I was wiping my tears now but my voice did not break, "You are the best thing that could ever happen to us. But if we don't tell you the truth, then we don't love you. From today on I will be free."

My mom had stood up, mumbled something about how everything she does is to help. If we did not want her help or if this was how we planned to insult her, she wanted to go back to Warri.

"Just change my ticket, you hear?" she finished and went into her room.

She did not come out till I left the next morning. For the first time in two weeks, I slept in my bed. I slept like a baby. The talk with mum had exhausted me. But in a strange way, it relieved me. I was lighter and clearer. I felt I had grown more mature overnight. And I knew there was no turning back. I made a mental note to check on a possible nanny and to call the airlines to change mum's ticket.

I really wanted her here with me to share my new-mom experiences, but I was resigned to whatever decision she made for herself. That was what boundaries meant; that I had to be okay with her decision, Just as I wanted her to be with mine. When I came back from work, I peered tentatively inside the house half expecting a scowling face and the now familiar tension I was now accustomed to. But instead, I heard singing and laughter.

"Nnoo o, Nwam. Welcome. Odafe ordered peppered fish from Africa market restaurant. Would you like some?" My mum was speaking to me; her eyes were looking at me warmly.

I did a double take. Was I dreaming?
She continued, "Please give me one monitor too. So, I can share the waking up time for baby with you and you can rest well"

`Then glancing at the TV, “Come and see this Oprah show. So funny.” She laughed heartily.

I stared in disbelief. I could recognize the closest thing to an apology after not having one all the years of my life. I felt free. Not just free to be me and do me but free to be my mother’s daughter: loved and outrageously cherished.

“Mummy, what day do you want me to change the ticket to?” I ventured, testing the veracity of the moment.

She turned my way and said “Don’t change it o. where am I going? Abi somebody cannot play with you again?”
That day, our relationship transcended to a mature, respectful one. Yes, I knew we would not always agree on everything in future, but it would be two adults talking this time with respect and love

I smiled, washed my hands and started devouring at the delicious peppery fish with my fingers, savouring the taste and licking my fingers

A DIFFERENT SET OF CIRCUMSTANCES

Church was still noisy and bustling after mass. With the customary goodbyes and hugs, women could be seen catching up effusively. Even though many would have seen each other, multiple times during the week at adoration, legion of Mary or at the Catholic Women's Organisation meetings. CWO members were dressed in their uniform; a royal blue gorge wrapper with *CATHOLIC WOMEN'S ORGANIZATION* printed around a circle, white poplin blouse, pristine and plain, with a double flapped round neck and slightly puffed sleeves. The crowning gele in the blue shade of the wrapper creatively tied in layers of folds, twists, and knots.

"Peace of the Lord be with you."
"And also with you."

The two women hugged, touching their chests and shaking hands in the timeless Catholic tradition. As they pulled apart, Belema asked "Have they come out?"

Doshima looked around, her sharp and small eyes flashing like a security guard's torchlight then she exclaimed with a look of relief, "See them under the tree."

They both started walking towards the tree as they chatted about the homily of the just ended Mass.

Belema, a beautiful, light skinned woman looked like she was once the belle of the town; her five-feet-ten strident gait portrayed her confidence. The slivers of silver in her hair were a reminder of the years that had passed and the wealth of experience one could glean from her.

Doshima was an opposite in many ways; she was about half a foot shorter but her small frame, the color of a ripe cocoa bore a womanly figure that curved in the right places. Her peal of laughter was gentle, softening her demure face. Belema was a step in front as usual; ready to marshal the troops when they approached the children.

Their nine children milled in a cluster. The girls, Obioma and Ujunwa, sat on a tree stump playing a palm-slapping and finger snapping game called 'My Mother Told Me'. The teenage boys: Emeka, Udoh and Arinze sat on the trunk of a car bobbing their head to some music emanating from the car. Their nanny clutched the hands of Kamsi and Kobi who were four and three years old respectively.

Obioma and Ujunwa, the gangly tweens, walked towards their mothers as they approached and promptly reached out to carry their purses as a sign of respect– as though carrying their purses a few yards further with would hurt their hands. They knew that not doing this would surely earn side-eyed looks from the adults in the vicinity, and when such acts of respect are learned early, they become a part of the subconscious.

"Come on kids. Let's go," Belema said.
"Ehen," added Doshima turning to face Belema, "Did he tell you?"
"What?" Belema started then it dawned on her and she tilted her head. "So, he is serious?"
"Yes o, my Sister, our husband indeed intends to take a third wife," Doshima confirmed.
"How can he? Look at all these children, what is he thinking?" Belema complained, "He mentioned it to me last week, but I thought he was playing."

“That’s an expensive joke o. Unfortunately, he means it,” Doshima responded.

Belema scoffed and sucked on her teeth, producing a hissing sign of discontent.

As they drove home, first navigating through the crowded bottleneck at the gate of the church and through the streets that seemed like one endless logjam with sellers hawking their wares in semi-permanent shanties, Belema thought back several years ago when she first met their husband. He was simply Ejike, before he morphed into this super important person with the title of Chief.

It was in the heat of the Nigeria-Biafra Civil War, and she was a staff nurse at a primary care centre where they treated virtually every case that was not critical. Families were always teeming in the waiting room and at the time, Belema could not think of a better way to help the efforts being put in than dedicating her time and energy to the helpless children. They were the reason she became a nurse, and it soon became apparent by the way parents requested for her when they brought their sick children.

On one of those days, a sister came to call her from the sleeping quarters, and she knew it had to be a serious case, as she had only slept for four hours after a late-night shift. The Day Clinic was fast becoming a full-fledged hospital, with more pediatric cases inundating them. Children were, inadvertently, the most impacted casualties of war.

When she got there, she saw him holding a toddler in his arms. He could have easily been a baby because of the seeming weightlessness but her trained eye deciphered the size of this flailing hand and his overall height to know this was an extremely sick three-year-old. The distended stomach was the clincher in the diagnosis, which of course, she would have to confirm with the resident doctor. Who always seemed to only agree with her diagnosis and did little checking. Maybe if he were here for more than a couple of hours a day, instead of hobnobbing with the military personnel.

As she reached for the baby, she noticed his strong big arms as they momentarily brushed against hers. His worried eyes, a sparkling shade of oatmeal, were piercing. His skin was the colour of the earth. His chest, she could not see, but it was rippling against his pristine olive-green army uniform. He smelled musky with the staleness of sweat, like he had been working his muscles hard for a long while.

“Come with me,” she said, heading inside and cradling the baby.
“Where is his mother?” She added glancing around.

Few fathers showed up here, and even fewer brought sick children by themselves.

“She is not here,” he said, gruffly.
“Is she...?”Belema asked, looking at him, sharply.
“No, she is not dead. She just... left.”
“Oh,” she responded, walking even more briskly to the examination room.
“What’s his name?”
“Emeka.”

As she placed him on the cold padded table, he started to struggle feebly.

“Oh Emeka, you are going to be okay, you hear?” she cooed. It was a forlorn attempt to get the sick child to calm. The sick child’s father impatiently instructed the child to stay put, with a brusque tone and pointing finger.

Belema turned and looked at him sternly and disappointingly with a quick shake of the head.

As she looked into Emeka's tired bulging eyes. She saw a flicker of life and started humming to him while examining him. "Jesus loves the little children, all the children of the world ..."

Emeka caved and let her examine him.

He ended up staying there for a whole month. In that time, Belema had come to learn a lot from Emeka's father, who visited almost daily for the first couple of weeks. Emeka's mother had left, abandoning her young son with his paternal grandmother, who was frail and sickly herself. The grandma had died shortly before he arrived from his station in Port Harcourt, and Emeka had been left with the neighbours, malnourished and starved; the poster child image of the Biafran children in a war that destroyed more within than without.

Ejike had to leave after a couple of weeks, and Belema offered to take care of Emeka like he was her own. By the time he returned in a couple of months, Emeka was plumping up and the energy was restored in his eyes. Belema never stopped thinking of Ejike while he was gone; they had developed an attraction and an easy fondness in those two weeks. She had felt obliged to take care of not just his son, but him as well.

His devotion to Emeka was what clinched it for her. When he came back to the station in Amauzo, they got married in a happy, small ceremony. Her parents could not attend because their hometown of Port Harcourt had been taken over by Nigerians at the time, and Biafran soldiers had to retreat. There was no travel in or out.

Six months later, Belema was pregnant with their first child, but she still went religiously to the clinic, working devotedly. It was one insanely hot afternoon that a stranger dropped by and altered everything. There was a knock on the door of their home. A woman stood out there with a baby on her back, looking up at her confused. The woman looked vaguely familiar. Her hair was wrapped with a scarf and she was dressed in a flowery dress. A wrapper cloth was tied firmly around her chest to secure the baby. Expectant though tired eyes travelled down to Belema's bulging stomach. Realization dawned and she started crying silently.

"What's the matter?" Belema inquired, walking towards her. She cried some more as Belema held her, "Come inside. Are you looking for someone? Is it Ejike, my husband?"

Emeka came up at that point and said, "Mummy!"

That was when the strange lady burst into tears. Still perplexed but concerned, Belema put her arms around her and led her into the sparsely furnished but neat apartment. That was fifteen years ago.

Doshima told Belema she ran away when she found out she was pregnant because Mazi Nna, Ejike's uncle, kept making advances towards her, threatening to "take it by force" if she did not cooperate. Ejike had been away for two months at the time without any communication. People were saying that a Biafran contingent had perished in the hands of the Nigerian soldiers and Ejike could have been in the troop. In addition, she knew she needed help with the new baby. So, she woke up early one morning, dropped Emeka with his grandmother, and left.

It broke her heart not to take him, she had said, but she knew the journey was fraught with danger. That was why she left. Belema's instincts and training took over. She comforted Doshima as she would any other distraught mother at the clinic with a dire case and offered to take the baby still strapped on her back. When she saw the yellowness in the baby's eyes, she took them straight to the clinic and there, nursed her back to health from jaundice.

When Ejike returned, he berated Doshima for leaving her son and abandoning their marriage and asked her to go back from whence she was coming. Doshima was rocking the baby with her son, on one hand, sobbing quietly on the other hand. Belema intervened that day. Looking back now she knew it was her nursing vocation that made her pity a mother (and her defenceless children) that had lost her family in the war with nowhere to go. Or maybe it was because she already saved one of Doshima's children once. She could not guarantee they would make it through the next ailment without proper medical care in the right environment. But she asked Ejike to let her stay that night and not raise his voice at her.

That was some fifteen years ago. They had all made a home beyond the war. They had worked out an effective system. Doshima and her children lived in one wing of the house while she lived in another with her children. It was not entirely strange to Belema. She grew up in a polygamous home. In fact, her stepmother had practically raised her when her mother died at childbirth. She had also been the one who pushed her to go to school. Under any other circumstance, she may never have supported being a second wife. But as it was, she had come into this by happenstance. Nothing was normal in wartime.

Doshima had cared for all the children, while she worked at the clinic. They were like sisters, except that Ejike spent half the week with Doshima and four nights with Belema. That was the deal. They had a system that worked; the children called both women 'Mummy' and others admired their family love.

So, for Ejike to say he wanted another wife was like a slap in the face. How could he want a third wife? Did he not see that having two wives was not his choice, and that if he had not been helpless, it would not have been? Those those were special circumstances that happened once in a lifetime. This was not the man she had lived with for almost the last two decades. The man she had literally, asked, no, told, to take his first wife back was now actively seeking out a new wife. She managed a mirthless chuckle as she reminisced on the early days.

She had steadily moved up in her career and hospital management until some investors approached her on a new healthcare project. Now she owned a twenty-five percent stake in that multimillion-dollar facility. They wanted the experience and credibility she had built in the region and the international community because of her work with indigent children. All she had required of them was to have an outreach arm for the helpless in society.

And so, she was well off and had supported Ejike's lobby for a chieftaincy title and a failed bid for some state elected position. Since then, he had gotten involved with the kind of men that always had a young lady, their daughter's age in their arms. Maybe this was him proving to them that he was one of them; but she knew better. He was not and no, she was not going to fund this lifestyle, much less a new wife.

Everything she had done, and all of her sacrifice and care were for the defenceless: the children, and Doshima – not for Ejike. Yes, she loved him, but she loved and protected the others. If he was going to go ahead, to marry another woman she would not be a part of it, sitting and smiling.

This was the line in the sand, and she was going to draw it, like all the other decisions that had brought her to this moment. She would ask him to leave of course; this house was owned by the hospital although she would be eligible to keep the house in seven years.

What about Doshima and the kids? She thought of them. She sat up and heard a knock on her room door. As she raised her head, she saw Doshima walk in, a silent strength exuding her petite frame.

She nodded at Belema and said, "I've been thinking, Sister. I will not do o. I am certain of it. What do we do?" Belema smiled and entered into a calm certainty that captured what words could not express. As long as they both agreed and worked together, their family would be fine.

A LINE IN THE SAND

The muscles of resilience grow stronger adversity, after adversity."
"If not us, then who?"

Driving on the way to the coastal town of Corpus Christi in South Texas, Victoria would glance at Kingsley and they would share those soppy, adoring glances that newlyweds shared. From time to time, one would reach out and hold the other's hand and give a warm squeeze as The Corrs crooned on the radio.

"I will run away with you.
Cause I... am falling in love with you.
No, never... I'm never gonna stop falling in love with you."

Between the bands, Cranberries and The Corrs, soft rock maintained that atmosphere of love for them. It was their warm place: their place of restoration and rejuvenation, their place of reminiscing and romance. The three-hour trip from Houston ended at the Hilton overlooking the lagoon downtown.

They did not bother to park in the garage. They pulled up at the valet's desk in front of the hotel lobby. Victoria leaned across the consul and kissed Kingsley smiling warmly with bright eyes, "Well done, Bae." she greeted him.

"Well, you helped me. Thanks, You!" he said, leaning back in to kiss her the second time.

He was wearing the cologne she got him as a just-because gift. Or was it for their fifth anniversary that just passed a couple of months ago? She could not tell now, but it made her feel so close to him. The valet was approaching their car, and they broke away, so Kingsley could grab their bags. Victoria stepped out with her glittery slippers, dressed in jeans shorts and a free-flowing, vacation-ready, peach chiffon blouse on her plus sized frame. She looked like the picture of a Bahamas tourist, who just stepped off a luxury yacht in her oversized glasses and flowing Indian hair extensions.

Bearing their backpack and rolling their hand luggage, Kingsley joined her with his arms around her. He was six feet to her five-foot frame and they walked inside. They were the picture of a couple in love. After checking in, they went upstairs to their 7thfloor ocean view room. There was champagne chilling in the ice bucket and chocolate-covered strawberries waiting on the table and rose petals scattered all over the bed and floor. They laughed and talked and drank, reminiscing on their days in college and their early years as broke immigrant students in America. Eventually, they came together, into each other's arms where they belonged, and made slow and steady love on the bed of roses.

A couple of hours later, they were freshened up and going for dinner at the romantic Marina restaurant on the pier. In a lovely little black shiny dress, Victoria looked delectable, draped on Kingsley's arms. He had cleaned up himself, looking dapper in burgundy chinos pants and a black suede jacket. They chose the five-course Chef Special and were given premium place by the window with the best water view.

The waiter, Raul, looked pleased as they considered his wine selection advice and offered to let them take a sip. He stood there as they swirled, smelled and sipped.

"You definitely know your wine." he said.

Oh yes, they liked wine and had learned the art on several wine tasting beats, they said, choosing the Fredericksburg Grapecreek vintage merlot to go with Victoria's petite filet and Kingsley's ribeye steak.

"Great choice," a gratified Raul commended them.
Then he asked, "What are we celebrating today, People?"

Kingsley and Victoria looked at each other and smiled. Not the warm, curvy, awkward grin but the pressed lip smile that carries more than it expresses.

"Life," Kingsley said.
"Life," echoed Victoria,
"...and the promise of tomorrow."

She raised her glass to Kingsley's and repeated, "To Life... and getting through this."

Raul, not fully comprehending mumbled, "Congratulations." and went back to the kitchen. The meals were sumptuous and plate after plate kept coming out in quick succession with the most delicious and delectable garnishes. For the finale, the chef himself came out of the kitchen. In tow was Raul with the raspberry cream cheesecake with chocolate ganache. On it was a sparkler whose light was sparkling with impatient intensity. The award-winning restaurant only had two couples by now. It was a Tuesday night in the school district, after all.

"Feliz Aniversario," announced the chef loudly.
Victoria and Kinsley waved no, laughing. It was not their anniversary.
He said, *"Buena Vida."* They all nodded in agreement at this consensus and clapped, laughing.

The Chef repeated the pivotal question Raul had asked them earlier. Victoria started and stopped. "You really want to know?"

Chef and waiter nodded.
"Go on," Kingsley urged her on.
"Our son just got diagnosed with autism. After two years of concern and despair. So... there." she finished, thrusting her hands in the air with a flourish.
They were standing, now unsure of their next step. What to say, what to do.
"It's okay," Kinsley said. "At least now we know we've got each other and can pull through this."

The chef and waiter never came out again after they left, mumbling apologies and explanations.

As they walked the pier back to the hotel, a short distance away, life had prepared them for this moment from their days on campus at the University of Port Harcourt in Nigeria.

Over a decade ago, they had met at the Faculty of Engineering in the incessantly long lines of fresher's teasingly called JAMBites queuing to register as new students after being admitted to the University. For some reason, those lines never seemed to move. The clerks took their time; others jumped the queues because of their connections or bribery. Man-know-man, the age-old syndrome of getting a leg up through your pedigree or alliances you paid for.

For Victoria and Kingsley, whose parents had no interest in alleviating the plight of their young children having to queue for whole days, they were stuck in that quadrangle. They shared an interest in books so while others talked and shouted and shoved, they stood in line, books to their faces and read while they edged on slowly.
Victoria first noticed him when she got to the end of her novel. They had been on the line then for five hours. It was their second day. She asked to borrow his book because she knew

she could not bear another minute without some escapism. Kingsley, all tall and lanky with the cutest smile said "Sure" and the rest was history.

They became an item for the rest of their college years. Kingsley talks about the first thing he noticed about her: perfectly sculpted square jaws. "Interesting face," he would call it. He was like that, an intellectual and logical person. Not one to say beautiful, if he meant interesting. He was one for facts and conviction.

Victoria was the optimist, the fair-weather, happy-go-lucky, expect-something-good kinda girl. They made quite the pair. And award after campus award gave them the title of 'Cutest Couple' Looking back, though they were not exactly the cutest, their longevity in a sea of false starts and breakups that plagues freshmen, must have stood out to someone.

It was a smooth run, their relationship. Full of steady infatuation and ease. So, when they experienced their first setback, it was newsworthy. They had gone to study at Lecture Hall 2 in Choba Park, in a university campus that dotted a three-mile radius. The East-West Road was a highway that passed through the large campus, separating the hostels from some of the lecture theaters. Students would walk across this major road several times a day without a dedicated pedestrian walkway or streetlights.

As they walked across, a car came from the adjacent road and without stopping before turning, swung into the road, headed right for them. It was truly a deer in the headlights moment except that they were actual people. They tried to move back out of the road but the car had the same thought and tried to swerve away as the inevitable crash happened. Some students who heard the screeching noise from a distance came running but by then, the hit and run driver had left the scene.

Kingsley's legs were broken and to this day, there is a metal plate in one of his legs while Victoria had internal bleeding and some broken ribs. They had to miss a whole semester to heal and recuperate. It was by far, the most difficult thing they had ever had to go through. When they eventually came to, they were in different hospitals and both insisted on being together, to their parents' perplexity.

Several surgeries and physical therapy sessions later, they went back to school, their infatuation had blossomed into something deeper. The kind of bond and maturity that is forged by adversity and overcoming. That was when they first realized, they would later say, that they would get married. They spent an extra year to make up for the semester they lost. Many nights were spent discussing their future and planning the life they would lead, how many children they would have. They even discussed budgets, based on future projected salaries. After building these castles in the air, they would find it ridiculous and have a good laugh.

Shortly after graduating from the Mechanical Engineering department, Kingsley got a scholarship to the University of Houston to study Oil and Gas Engineering. Victoria joined a year later at Texas Southern University in the same city. They both got jobs in the oil and gas sector and got married at a lavish event with their friends and family in Galveston, on the beach.

They had planned to have a baby almost immediately. In those days, they had curated the names of their three kids and the years they would be born in the matter-of-fact way that plans on paper are. Fate had other plans. After two years and the babies were not coming, Victoria, not one for dilly-dallying, added action to her faith and prayers. A barrage of fertility tests and several doctor consultations later, the verdict was that everything seemed normal and there was no reason why they should not have babies.

So, when baby Ryan came along after three years of waiting, she nicknamed him 'Faith's Child' because he came when they had nothing else but hope. Six months later, she noticed she was pregnant again a little baby girl, Regina, this time.

They were so blessed. God had been good to them. Kingsley was getting promoted at work; Victoria got a new, more flexible role. They were the dream family till adversity struck once again.

In coping with work, a pregnancy and new birth, it was hard to notice Ryan's regression. It started slowly; he would not respond to his name or make eye contact. Not when they played with him or spoke to him, he would look anywhere but in their eyes. He would say "Dada" or "Mama" when he was one year old but at two, he had no other words and would not even call his parents. Having never had any other babies as an example, it was easy to miss these signs until Kingsley's mum came to visit from Nigeria. Victoria's mum had come to help when Ryan was a baby and now it was the other Grandma's turn.

Grandma was concerned. Children in Nigeria would have started talking since their first birthday and speaking in sentences by 18months. What was the matter? She tried to sing to make him happy but he just fixated on a wall away from everyone else or played with his toys in a strange way.

He would take out the Lego blocks and line them up instead of building a structure; he would upturn the toy car and spin its wheels instead of rolling the car functionally. The one that broke Mama's heart was him not wanting to be carried or hugged. He cringed and fought when anyone tried to hold him close.

To help him interact with his peers, they decided to enrol him in a preschool. At first, he was a pleasure to all the teachers and caregivers who loved the non-biters and the ready-eaters, who ate everything put in front of them. But the complaints started coming in, he would not play with his classmates or sit still to do any work. In addition, he would not communicate in any way.

But he was incredibly healthy otherwise and so the next doctor visit after 18months came at two years old when he was due for his wellness visit and shots. After reviewing the development checklist that they had filled, the doctor announced to Victoria and Kingsley that he was concerned and referred them to specialists.

Within a month, Ryan had seen an ear, nose and throat doctor, a pediatric neurologist and a developmental pediatrician for several evaluations and assessments. Victoria took time off work to care for her son and with Kingsley; they attended every appointment, together. The same way they had always been, that was how they were going to go through this. The assessments were complicated by Ryan's responses or lack of it.

To test hearing, he had to be sedated and underwent a procedure where they checked his brain responses instead of his physical responses to sound because even when he heard sound, he would not turn to look. There was the excruciating EEG, another procedure where small pads like placed around Ryan's head with wires. He looked like an Ichie, a village chief, with the sock-like cap holding all those wires in place and like Rapunzel, they intertwined in a 2ft long string to the transmitter that recorded the brain waves that would tell if he was having seizures.

Desperately, he tried his hardest to remove the wires the whole day, tugging at them on every turn. Just as diligently, his parents and grandma took turns watching over him and distracting him till he finally slept. The sight of Ryan, with wires and head pads, a tug at their loving hearts.

Victoria was strong through this, focused on action and solutions but when the doctor announced that they did not get the results because he possibly moved around a lot till it disconnected, she broke down and let a gut-wrenching groan.

She could go through anything and not be moved but for her son, the impossibility of taking his place was not something she could deal with.

It made her think of her mother in-law. She was a stoic woman, seemingly without emotions or at least, the demonstration of them. Yet, Kingsley had said this was only the second time in his life he had seen her cry. The first was when she lost her dad. Grandma would cry and ask God to make her deaf instead of her grandson.

But on and on, from testing center to consultants, they went, seeking answers that could not be found. The final one was the MRI scan (Magnetic Resonance Imaging) to check for abnormalities in his brain. An adult could take this procedure anywhere from 15 to 90 minutes as an outpatient, but Ryan had to be admitted to the hospital. He would require sedation to bear staying still in such an enclosure,

The day before the final meeting with the paediatric neurologist to review the comprehensive results of several tests, they were having their nightly tea on the back patio. When Kingsley asked if she had meetings for the next work day, she had not suspected his plans. He went in and came back out and said "Tadaa! I just booked a trip to Corpus Christi."

She looked up quizzically, still trying to understand, he explained, "Don't worry, I have spoken with Mummy, she will be okay with the kids for the next two nights. They will be okay."

She smiled. "Whatever happens, happens... we will be okay."

The next day at the clinic, the doctor gravely pronounced the final diagnosis as ASD "Autism Spectrum Disorder. They looked at each other and pressed their held hands even tighter. Went home, got their bags, bade goodbye to their son's grandma and headed for Corpus Christi.

That was two nights ago. A weekend in Corpus Christi had rejuvenated them and helped them recharge for the journey ahead. If it were possible, they were more in love than ever before. But this was a more desperate and mature kind of love. They had grown overnight.

As Kingsley went to go get the car after checkout, Victoria walked over on the pier towards the sea, which was particularly restless that day. With wind in her hair, hands in her pockets and peace in her heart, she was reminded of the scripture from their devotional study that morning at their usual prayer time:

"We stand fearless at the cliff's edge...
Courageous in seastorm and earthquake,
Before the rush and roar of oceans,
The tremors that shift mountains,
GOD is our refuge"
- Psalm 46:1-3

Ahead of them lay even more tests, possible seizures and sleepless nights. Speech, occupational and applied behavioral therapy. Soon, they would be considering guardianship and trustees for their estates, legal technicalities that many of their peers did not yet have to consider or ever would. The many alternative medicine options and therapies they would consider in exploring a cure. The judging eyes, and thoughtless questions by both well-meaning and insensitive people.

Even though they had been impacted by this condition, that no one knew where it came from or how it went, they were determined to be okay. To keep fighting for their little boy who deserved the best in life, to be there for their daughter who did not deserve to be short-changed and most of all, to faithfully hold the center of this family. The center was the love they shared that had weathered many storms with many more brewing on the horizon.

They had drawn a line in the sand with this one: autism on one side, Victoria and Kingsley on the other, and that was how it would always be.

MY MADAM'S OGA

You can hear the drip, drip, drip of the faulty tap above the faint church speakers in the distance. The megaphones are announcing prayer time, but the constant dripping is louder than whatever sounds you can hear from outside our gates. It is the sound of silence. It is the sound that follows my Oga beating my Madam. The way the gateman beats his stubborn children if they misbehave. That is how he beats Madam, like a child.

I have always wondered why she cradles her head in her hands: one hand in front and the other at the back of her head.

Maybe, it is to protect her face. Madam is so fine; she has that raw African beauty with pointed nose and full lips. Madam is fine sha. Especially, when she makes up and she is going to one of her churches. She does not just go to one church o; she goes to many men and women ministers for special prayers so that Oga will change.

I know because she told me. One time, I even followed her to one because we stopped after going to the market, and as we drove home, she told me in the car.

"You won't believe what that Pastor told me. He said I should go and tell his family members or people he respects." Then, she laughed but her eyes did not narrow like a happy person.

"He wants me to go and embarrass my husband before his family and friends so that he will kuku kill me. I just said 'Thank you Sir,' and left. Instead of him to just pray for me, he was saying what a pastor should not have said."

Another day, she told me she cut off Aunty Efua who always brought chin chin-chin and puff-puff for the children and me anytime she visited. I like that aunty, she is a good woman who cares about Madam. And she does not shout at me like Madam's other friends.

"How can Efua advise me to confront my husband? She thinks we are like Ghanaians who behave like Oyinbo? Please o, we have our traditions." Madam told me.

Madam always reminds me of the time she brought her uncle to come and talk to Oga to stop beating her all the time. That was after he dislocated her arm and she had to go to a local orthopaedic to put the bone back in place. Uncle Weneka came and he and Oga sat under the mango tree in front in our compound. At first, their voices were quiet, as though they were discussing a secret; but I knew the whispering would not be for long, because Oga is like the stone in a catapult that is about to be fired. In fact, if he is too quiet, the shout will be higher when he is released.

That's how Oga started shouting at Uncle Weneka.

"Did I not pay her bride price? Uncle, if not for the respect I have for you, I would have asked you to leave. You people keep interfering with me and my wife's business, o kini?" He turned towards the house and shouted even more "Huoma, do you see what you are causing? If I handle you this evening..."

This warning always preceded the beatings.

Of course, Madam who does not know herself went outside to go and separate fight. Me? I held my hand over my mouth, the way I do when I know what is about to happen. That's how she went to kneel near Oga.

"Emenike, don't be angry now. I just wanted Uncle to...."

As she was talking, she was holding Oga's leg. That was how he pushed her. His hand must be very strong because Madam fell on the ground.

Uncle Weneka stood up and pointed his finger at Oga. His voice was vibrating; he was angry.

"How dare you? In my presence? So, you cannot even show me respect?"

Oga did not even answer him, he was just drinking his tombo on the tree stump we use as stool. Uncle asked Madam to stand up and follow him.

"When you are ready to change your ways, come and see us in Elele to reconcile with your wife. It is forbidden for you to put your hand on somebody's daughter in the presence of her father." He told Oga.

"When you finish, you leave my compound, you hear." Oga said before he carried his glass and walked away. His leg even brushing against Madam as she was there crying on the floor. Uncle tried to raise her up, but she refused o. She said that she cannot leave her husband. Every time she tells me this gist, she always says she cannot listen to anybody that brings temptation for her to leave her marital home.

I think she forgets that she has told me these things several times because she has not stopped. I hear them every day and always in the same sequence. The only days when she does not talk to me is when I burn beans, and she is not happy with me. I know she thinks it is punishment, but I wish I could burn food more often, so she can let me be for a couple of days. Now that she has cut off many of her friends, she thinks I am her friend.

I am not. I am Barile, the children's nanny. I have also become the maid since Oga told Madam's sister Lemchi to go back to the village when Madam went to her shop. He said Aunty Lemchi was advising his wife wrongly and turning her mind against him. Aunty Lemchi is a nice lady; she can cook the whole day and not get tired. At least when she was here, Madam had somebody else to talk to. Now, it is only me.

I just passed my WAEC and JAMB examinations that Madam paid for me to write. Madam is kind; other madams will not pay because they do not want their nannies to go, but Madam is a good woman, so she encouraged me to sit for the examinations. My madam went to school. She says she and Oga were classmates at the University of Science and Technology. That is why I am surprised at how Oga treats her like those cow owned by Fulani herdsmen.

If I go to big school like university, nobody will know me again. I will be carrying my shoulder up, the way those women at the bank tellers do. I will wear suit and work somewhere important. I will never let anyone treat me the way oga treats my madam.

The thought of my future always puts a smile on my face.

My smile does not stay on my face when I think of the children; Uche, Nyema, and Chimso. I will really miss those children. Who will even take care of them? Madam is too unsteady for them. They need a strong person who will teach them and still be firm with them. She is no longer as sound as she used to be. Sometimes, when she is not repeating stories to me, she will be saying some stories that I know Oga fed her: stories of how she is a bad wife, or that if she is a good wife, her husband will not be beating her.

One time, she even said she was the one who started the fight and that she punched him first. Madam that does not have 'power'? Thank God I was there that day, or I may have believed her. Oga lied to her until she believed it. Now, she tells it as her own story. I wish she would listen to the pastor or her friend or Uncle Weneka and leave this place.

The dripping came back to my mind. The silence is still there. I can hear madam softly now; she is crying in her room. Oga marched out of the house like a king after all the blows I heard through the walls. When the blows became too much, I shut the door and increased the volume of the television, so the children will not hear. I think Uche, the oldest child, who is 4 now knows. Though her eyes were on the show they were watching, she was quiet. Then, she has started sucking her thumb. As a baby, she never sucked her thumb. I did not even know that children could suck their thumbs after they have grown.

I waited till they all slept off before I went to Madam's room, to help her in any way that I could. "Madam, I bring tea. Please let me bring it inside for you. It will help, Ma."

She was crying harder so I went inside. Chai, if you see Madam, it will touch your heart. Half of her face had turned black, so I knew he punched her face. If you see Oga setting his hands when he wants to beat Madam ehn, you will think he is at the motor park, fighting with his fellow men. Blood was flowing from a wound on her head, and all over her hands were marks, belt marks. Oga used his belt and maybe turned it on the head, which was why Madam had the injury on the head.

"Ha, Madam! Let's go to the hospital. Please Ma. You need treatment."
"Don't worry, Barile. It will get better." she said through her swollen and bruised lips.

This was not like other times. I do not know if she could hear me, but I started trying to get her outside so that we could go to the hospital. I would tell the gateman's wife to watch the children. I do not want Madam to die in this house. As we were walking towards the door, Oga entered the house. Immediately, Madam slumped off me to the floor, crying and begging, *"Biko,* Emenike, *biko."*

"Did I not tell you not to leave that room?" he screamed.

I could see that he had gone to the pharmacy to buy some Panadol and some plasters. He turned to me then, and his face was like the devil's own, angry and twisted. If you see the way he slapped me... in my life, nobody has ever hit me like that, not even my father. The force made my head hit the wall in the walkway. It hurt as though I fell on the floor with my face, and I inched the next few feet to the adjacent kitchen, trying to get away.

"Oh! Barile, you have grown now." Oga said, coming behind me. "You that I helped to take from your father, our company driver, to help your life? You now want to disobey my instructions in this house? Are you mad? Are you crazy?"

Each question was followed by a kick.
How can anybody endure this? I thought I would die.

All the time, Madam was saying, "Leave her, please. I asked her to come and help me."

"Don't worry. I will teach both of you a lesson." Oga thundered. As he reached for me again, I instinctively snatched the porcelain flowerpot hanging decoratively on the wall turned and threw it at him. It struck him squarely in the face. He screamed, clutched his face, staggered, and fell. While he was still shouting and cursing, I gathered myself to stand up.

Meanwhile, Madam was already at his side.
"What have you done?!" She was wailing.
"Call for help. I need a doctor. My head o. My head o. See blood!" Oga screamed. He seemed amazed that there was

blood in his head, the way he kept touching it and looking at it.

I ran into my room, collected my handbag with my salary of three months that I had been saving for school and ran out of the compound. Before I left, I still asked Madam to follow me, but she remained there with her battered body, trying to tend to her husband's wounds. I knew she would not stand up, and I do not know what would make her leave him, maybe death? I did not stay to find out.

I said a prayer for the children. I love them, and I pray that God will deliver them from this house.

I didn't go back to my parents' house. I ran to my auntie's house where no one would think of coming to search for me, to stay for a while after I broke Oga's head. I knew he would come for me; he would not just let this matter go. Oga threatened my poor father for days with an arrest but after a while, he had to let go. I knew someone had pleaded and subsequently paid the price for my imminent punishment. It was none other than my Madam.

A few months later, I saw Gateman's wife at Diobu Market at Mile 1, she told me that Oga is now blind in one eye and is to undergo a surgery on the other one; Madam is still taking care of him, and that she does not hear shouting and beating like before, anymore. She also said that Aunty Lemchi has come back and is now the one taking care of the children.

I felt a bit ashamed when I caught myself smiling, but I stopped and asked about her about her own children. Of course, she started pumping me with stories – half of which I would never remember.

"Stay well o" and "Greet Madam for me," I said after the chat, before I turned and walked away, hopping from stone to stone, down the swampy obstacle course that is Mile 1 Market, when it rains.

THE SAGE

My heart started pumping when I saw the letter with the crisp blue and white logo of the World Economic Forum.

"Oh my goodness! Oh my goodness! Oh my goodness!" I screamed in rising crescendo as I read the words, "...accepted as a Global Leadership Fellows Programme..." I let out a loud shout as I did the running-man dance in our small, quaint living room.

Segun came running down the stairs of our two-bedroom townhouse.

“Honey I got the fellowship!” I screamed some more.

He looked perplexed, so I shoved the letter in his hands as I continued my dance. I could not believe it. I mean, I know I wanted it; but this was my life’s career goal, to become a fellow at a global organisation. The moment became overwhelming, and I fell to my knees with tears streaming down my face as I praised God in that age-old chorus.

“Thank you, thank you, Lord,
Thank you Lord. Thank you Lord
For everything you have done.”

I was truly caught up in the moment else I would have realised that Segun did not join me in this euphoria. At that time, however, it was the farthest thing on my mind; but I heard him say he was going to get the children from school, which was where I was headed when the letter dropped through the pigeonhole in the door.

Oh my parents! My sisters. Pastor... everyone would be so happy for me, I thought.

Sure enough, every phone call thereafter was filled with “Congratulations!” and “I knew you would get it.”

"How big of a deal is this?" My younger sister asked me on the family group call.

"It's only the highest fellowship a policy advocate could aspire for. No big deal—"

"Ah, you know me I don't know book o. You are the first-class people."

We laughed together. "Well, Sis I'm so proud of you. You inspire me."

My dad and mum blessed me afterwards, "It shall be well with you. You have made us so proud."

Their prayers absolutely made my day.

If anyone told me that I would have my dream career in advocacy on a global scale, I would have doubted them. Though I volunteered with the student arms of global organisations like Junior Achievement and United Nations after I graduated from the University of Nigeria, Nsukka, with a first class in Economics, this fellowship is still a surprise.

Segun and I graduated from the same set, and he sparred across me in debates at our faculty. We were brilliant, we were visionaries, and we were going places. After graduation, I worked for the government in the Ministry of Women Affairs. My role entailed my writing to international organisations to seek grants. The job paid little, but I gained invaluable exposure and knowledge.

I was on course to senior levels with my track record of outstanding results and influence with stakeholders when Segun got a scholarship to Queens University, Belfast. It was a difficult choice, but I knew he needed the kids and me by his side while he completed his PhD. I had helped him complete the applications for admission and then the scholarship. Since his career had suffered a delay, it was important that he got the scholarship. This will, in a way, redeem his career and self-esteem.

Segun's career had a shaky start when we first left college. His attempted master's degree after graduation resulted in a postgraduate diploma because he had some issues with his supervisor, he said. I encouraged him until he got a job at the College of Science which he decried as "just a step higher than a secondary school". His ambition was to lecture at a university.

As my career blossomed, I knew he needed a pick-me-up. What wife blazes ahead without her husband? Moreover, I noticed his lack of enthusiasm for my work. I knew I had to help him, and I started looking for doctorate programmes abroad. Dutifully, I saved up money and quit my job to go with him when the semester started.

My boss at USAID tried to keep me working part-time in Nigeria for half the year, but Francis is big on loyalty, and I already gave my word. I wanted to be all in, so I paused my career for my husband. The sacrifice was painful, but necessary.

For the last three years, I have been the devoted wife, taking care of our six- and nine-year-old daughters. Segun's academic papers have also been my business, so I wrote widely and reviewed extensively. When his scholarship stipend was reduced, I took up call centre jobs to make up money for our upkeep. Those were difficult times, but I took the PhD as the current marriage project that must not suffer. *Of course, if not me, then who?* My job was to support, and I was there for it.

We had our future planned; we were going to return to Nigeria where he would get a university lecturer position, and I would return to the non-profit and advocacy space; and we would ride to the peak of our careers. That was the plan but recently, Segun began to consider remaining in Europe if he got a job in academia; so we hedged out bets, we would both look for jobs in Europe in the final year of his doctorate.

I started applying for both of us since that was my forte. When I told him I would shoot my shot and go for global entities like the United Nations, World Trade Organisation, and World Economic Forum, he laughed and said, "Let's see what happens."

What did I have to lose? I thought.

That was months ago.

That evening, after the euphoria of the news and the children were in bed, Segun and I had our nightly tea as we wound down the day.

"So, they want me to resume in two months in Geneva. I have been thinking of options."

"I don't think you can take this job o, Jemaima." His words ran me cold.

"I don't understand. Is that a joke, Segun?"

"How will I follow you all the way to Geneva? I am still wrapping up, and you know I have to be available for job interviews."

"We will make it work now, like we've always done. It's just a flight away if you need to come back. Plus, it's just for one year.

The experiences will open doors for me anywhere. Haven't we discussed all these before?"

This conversation was not going the way I planned it. A bottle of wine was chilling in the fridge, and I had even made oven spicy suya for the would-be private celebration.

"So you want me to follow you to Geneva? It won't happen."
"Francis, this is not fair. I don't understand you. Let's discuss later, please. Now is for celebration"
"We are not discussing anything. I have made up my mind. We are not going. Look for a job around here."

It was getting ridiculous.

"But you are not sure you will even stay here in Belfast, and you don't have any interviews lined up yet."
"Oh, you want to insult me now, right... that I don't have a job? In fact, I am done with this conversation. Forget about that job if you still want this marriage."

He stormed off, and I sank even lower into the couch staring intently at nothing, aghast at the direction the conversation had taken. How did this all go so wrong? Just how?

Following that, our home had become a ghost town; and we barely spoke to each other. Several people tried to intervene on my behalf, but Francis was not yielding. He would state that he did not support me taking this job, and that he was not moving to Geneva, under any circumstance. He also refused to consider an academic job there. He remained stubborn and resolute, yet he had the gall to call me stubborn.

Sometimes, I get so mad that I felt I could punch through a wall; at other times, hot tears overwhelmed me as I contemplated his meanness. Yes, I was now convinced that he was deliberately thwarting my goals.

The many options I presented before him got thrown out in an argument or simply met his wall of silence; and he moved to sleeping on the couch in our tiny study. He knew what this fellowship meant to me from our days in college. He knew the aspiring young woman he fell in love with.

A week to the acceptance deadline, I became desperate. Our union was supposed to be a marriage of partners and sacrifices on both ends. It was now my turn, and it was not looking like I would get my own opportunity.

My dad's intervention was the final straw that broke the camel's back. After three weeks of this impasse, my dad (convinced that he would listen to him) offered to come with my mother with me to Geneva so they could help with the children. This way, Segun could stay back in the United Kingdom to interview for jobs.

"Respectfully Sir, I don't tell you how to run your own home." he obstinately said to my dad before asking for his decisions to be respected.

Respected? Was he respecting me, his wife?

I was livid when my mum told me. The funny thing was that Segun's family was solidly behind him. His sister already advised me to stay if I wanted to keep my home.

"Is it because of a job, you want to lose your family?" She asked.

At my wits end in church that weekend, my pastor, a middle-aged Ghanaian with the sweetest demeanour and the wisest words, came up to me in the coffee and biscuits get-together we hold after service. He and his wonderful Jamaican wife, who had become mother to all the international families, had been married over thirty years.

“So when do you leave, Jemaima?” Pastor Kofi always called my name with his Twi accent that made the “J’ sound like “Ch”.
“Where?” I asked in a haze.
“Geneva, of course.”

It was only when he put an arm on my shoulder that I felt the tears on my face. I had been fighting so much that the slightest prodding had unravelled me. He and his wife comforted me that morning and asked to see Segun and me. I wondered why I had not thought of them earlier. They were one of the few people Segun esteemed, especially as our pastor is also a professor at the university.

I had not been happy in so long, and I knew there was no path to happiness in staying in Belfast and rejecting this opportunity. I would be resentful and bitter. How would that serve my marriage? Yet if I went, I would be abandoning my marriage.

Pastor Kofi reached out to Segun, and though I was not convinced that the man of God could influence anything, we both went to the meeting, anyways.

We started out with the standard arguments.

"Why can't you be happy taking care of the children and supporting me? Other women would be happy to stay at home." Segun asked me.

"But then I would be someone else. That's not who you married, Francis. You knew my passions and talents. You know my life's goals and dreams."
"Yes, but you are married now."
"I did not make a vow to sacrifice my dreams on your altar!" My voice was rising now.

Pastor Kofi soon decided that he had heard enough, so he calmed us down and set some ground rules: we were both going to have our turns, while he asked the questions.

I did not know what I was expecting, but Pastor Kofi sat there with a smile on his face as he listened to Segun talk about how his career came first, and he was not supportive of the job, and how I was the woman and should follow his lead.

Twice, I interjected to refute his claims, but Pastor Kofi shook his head.
"Your turn will come. Let him finish speaking," Pastor Kofi said.

In my mind, I started tuning out. This was a lost cause. Whose side did I think the pastor would take? Then, I noticed that Pastor Kofi was not only listening to Segun but also asking clarifying questions.

"What makes you say that?" Pastor Kofi asked him.
"Well, I feel like it's her duty to make sacrifices for this family." Segun insisted.
"Interesting," he stroked his white beard and paused. "So, tell me what that looks like?"
"She should support me anywhere I go. She should take care of the family. That is all I ask of my wife. If not, why else are we married? I am the husband."
"Right, right. So where are you going, so she can follow you?" Segun looked a little shaken by this question.
"I am still applying for jobs. When I have it, we should be moving there."
"What Jemaima is saying is that she wants to go and return as soon as you get a job. With your plan, won't that work?
Already, she feels that you are not supportive of her career."
I glanced at Francis; he was beginning to shift in his seat.

"Hmmmn! Pastor, it's not as if I don't want her progress. If the job were here, I will not mind, but I cannot bear to be away from my children that long. I want to take care of them and pray with them every night. It is important that they see their father daily"

He was beginning to sound petulant. Yes, he was good with the girls, especially since we moved from Nigeria where the girls had a nanny. But he could pray with them over the phone and we could plan to see every month.

"Pastor, if she wants to go, I'm not stopping her. She would just have to go without the children."
"Why would you even say that?" I asked, shocked. My girls meant everything to me. They were a part of my every day.
"Hold on one moment." Pastor Kofi said, turning to Segun. "So she can go without the children?"
"Yes. If she can go without them, let her go. My children will remain here. I am their father."
"Thank you very much, Segun," Pastor Kofi said. "I am glad we could reach a consensus."
I was a little confused. Surely the man of God was not...

"You have heard your husband. He is a great father. You can go alone and focus on your fellowship. I would advise you come as often as you can to visit, but don't worry too much, they will be in safe hands.", he turned to Segun, "My wife and

I will check in with the family and babysit the girls whenever you have an interview."

I began to understand.

"Yes. He is a good dad, Pastor. I know he can handle the girls. I will go to Geneva."

Immediately, I turned to Segun and threw my arms around him.

"Thank you for making my dreams come true, *Oko mi*. God bless you."

He sat there in my arms, rigid as the chair.

IF-IT-WERE-ME SYNDROME

My name is Nadia, a businesswoman and mother to two super amazing children and until recently, wife to Kenneth. No one who walks alone gets very far in life. We all need someone... anyone who would always have our backs and be our solace when the storm comes. Well, I have mine in my smart, crazy, multifaceted and loyal Soul-Sisters.

Status, religion and ethnicity are the least of our worries, Infact it adds a distinct and special flavour to our friendship. We all attended the same secondary school at Federal

Government Girls College, Abuloma. Back then, the unity schools were the melting pot of Nigeria, with students from virtually every state in the nation. It was a cultural feast as well as the making of young minds and eternal friendships. The kinds forged through being there for trials and triumphs in life's stages.

We were not just classmates in Mrs Nwosuagwu's class, we were house mates in same dormitory, Lavender House. With the advent of messenger groups, we found ourselves again and carried on our sisterhood through BlackBerry and now, WhatsApp. We share and we care, laugh and then cry, we rant but also encourage, we hail and we yab and sometimes, we even judge. One thing is for sure, all advice we share is from our perspectives and it takes a discerning person to sift through the "if-it-were-me" words of wisdom. Bring one problem to the group and the responses are as unique and outrageous as each individual.

This last year has been particularly difficult for me but my community was my safety and a large part of my healing. I have been through the storm, but I was not alone, no. My Soul Sistas were there to see me get through unscathed. These are from the chats we shared from when I first found out my husband was cheating.

6 Months Ago

NADIA: "Sistas, I am so devastated. I think Kenneth is cheating on me. I saw some text messages on his phone where he was chatting and sexting with a lady. I feel like my heart is torn from my chest. I don't know who else to turn to. I don't know what to do..."

MARY: "Ah, God forbid o, Nadia. We reject it in the name of Jesus. The devil is trying to destroy families. Not when God is on the throne. Have you been praying and fasting specifically for your husband? Look we are the ones who build them up. We will settle this thing spiritually. I join with you in prayer this morning to build a hedge around your home. The battle is The Lord's."

NJIDEKA: "Mary, wetin concern God inside again? Was it a threesome with God? Look, let me tell you, men are dogs! If not for children, who will marry them? That's why I always tell all of you to have exit plans. Do you have your vex-money? If not, start arranging yourself sharp-sharp make man no carry you see road. I don't trust any man and neither should you. My sista Nadia, clean your eyes and let's begin to plan so you won't be caught off-guard."

BUKOLA: "Ah Lagos Girls! Njideka, they are not dogs... it's the Jezebels that won't let them rest. The temptation is too much. See single women everyday dressing skimpily and flirting without shame, even married women. They are not safe: from bank to work even to church, they are everywhere. This is why I don't let any woman near my husband. Not even his sister. I don't trust anybody"

IVIE: "What is happening here? Why am I just seeing this? Kenneth dey craze? What rubbish? We go burst im brain for here. Have you broken his windscreen? Na to do am strong tin... men only listen to a crazy woman. Bukola, which Jezebels? Any Lagos girl that comes after my husband, I go beat shege commot from her head. Nadia, my love, I have told you before that you are too calm. My sister, pele. But don't cry too much, let's go and handle business. Where does the prostitute live? I am coming with you..."

INIOBONG: "Ah don't do that one o, please... Ivie, you are too violent, this advice is not good. Let's all calm down. You are a married woman: beating her or disrespecting your husband will only expose your shame for the whole world to see. My sister, Nadia, look let me tell you, everybody has their own but nobody will tell you. If I am not your friend, I will not tell you the truth. Single mother life is hard, how will you cope? Will you let one small girl win? Everything is packaging. Just ignore and move on, for the sake of the children. At the end of the day, that's what matters"

AISHA: "Iniobong, thank you o, for calling for calm. Let's be calming down. At the end of the day, we have to be introspective and reflect. Nadia, I am not saying this to hurt you but Kenneth has been faithful these four years you have been married and he never cheated. So why now? What is happening in your home and in your marriage that is causing him to go outside? Is he getting enough sex and attention or have the children taken over all your time? Remember, he is a man who needs attention. I will advise you to ignore that text and kill him with love. Serve him good food and perform in the other room. He will soon forget the other woman"

PREYE: "Nadia, are you okay? Please take care of you. You come first. Take a couple of days off if you need to. We are here for you. Please don't listen to any advice that does not resonate with you. Soul Sistas have come again! Can we just be there for Nadia at this time? All this advice sef... Nadia, at the end of the day, you will make the right decision for you and your children that will give you peace of mind. So sorry you have to go through this. Warm hugs and squeezes."

2 Months Ago

NADIA: "Sistas, I'm done!!! I am leaving Kenneth. The cheating has become unbearable. Yesterday, I walked in on him in our bedroom with our neighbor. Thank God the children were not back from school. I just came to pick up some goods for my shop. The humiliation is too much, I don't think I can continue..."

MARY: "Sister Nadia, endure, it's always darkest before dawn. You can get through this God knows why he exposed him to you so he can stop. Please give no place to the devil. There is nothing God cannot do. If only we stay in the place of faith and prayer, we will receive our breakthrough. Remember again, your two beautiful kids. Do you want them to grow up without a father?"

NADIA: "No Mary, I don't want them to grow up with an unfaithful and irresponsible example of a father. Have we not been praying together? All these months yet he has gotten worse. He has broken his word too many times yet he even goes to church more than me. The Bible says to watch and pray. Let me be praying for him from afar and watch to see if any change before we can talk about reconciliation"

BUKOLA: "Nadia, I am so sorry you had to see that. It's not easy to see another woman reap where you have sown. Please focus on the enemy. Those girls are the enemies. Maybe if you can move to another part of Lagos or even another state, the temptation won't be that bad. I don't believe Kenneth is a bad man, maybe it's his weakness. Again, keep shielding him. Delete all their numbers from his phone and monitor him.

Don't abandon your home because of these Jezebels. You have put in a lot into this marriage"

NADIA: "Bukola, did they all rape him? Or is he the finest man in Lagos? Four different girls now that I know of in the last one year. Did they all rape him? I am tired of accusing the girls. He is the common denominator. If Lagos girls want him, let them take please. I will not spend the rest of my days as a detective with the person who I should trust the most. I cannot fight. They can have him"

NJIDEKA: "See my babe don sharp o. Sis that's what I was trying to tell you. These men will enjoy your youth and spit you out like udara seed. I hope you have arranged yourself. Don't tell him how much you are making, your secret bank account. I just dey look as you dey mumu before, please change all those landed property to your name.

NADIA: "Njide, I'm telling you. I want to talk to my lawyer and see what I can do because God knows I did not marry Kenneth for his money. Marriage was not a business for me. I refuse to have to lie to him or hide any money. When I married him, he was a pauper! Now the money is rolling in, his character is out of the window. No one can talk to him.

Thankfully, we both own the company together. The children and I should be okay. I just hope the courts rule speedily so we can discuss assets. No amount of money will help me get used to cheating.

IVIE: "Me nor understand you o... naim make I like Warri girls. Because we dey craze. I begged you that I want to carry this fight but you refused. You can't be too gentle in this life, people will walk over you. Sha tell me what you want: if you want to stay, we can handle business and if you want to leave, everything in that house must first be broken to pieces. Nadia, you are too nice... You don't deserve this at all.

NADIA: "Ivie, you know me... I don't have power. Fight o, I can't fight. Even shout, I can't shout anymore. I cannot live in a warzone. If Kenneth is done, there is no need to fight for him."

AISHA: "Waiyo! When you did not mention this all these months, I thought you have found his mumu button again. Nadia, are you sure? We can still try some things; let's not give up. There is still kayamata and tiger nut. Does he still eat at home? In fact, I will pay for spa, hair and nails for you. When his eyes see you, he will forget everything else. Service your man, don't let him go"

NADIA: "Aisha, leave that thing. I am a size 8, sexy with a great figure. The same way Kenneth has always said he liked me. The girls I even saw were nowhere near me but he still followed them. Like how?"

INIOBONG: "Oh my goodness. Please I hope you haven't told anybody. Please don't. We are your safe space but not everybody is looking for your good. Some people are expecting this news so they can gloat but God pass them. Girlfriend wears some makeup, buy yourself some clothes and enjoy yourself, by yourself. When Kenneth finishes playing, he will come back"

NADIA: "I hear you Sis, I hear you. But this charade has to end somewhere, doesn't it? What's the use wearing co-uniforms and smiling in public when we have deep-seated issues? I will keep you guys posted. I appreciate you, Sistas"

PREYE: "Sis, you must be devastated. I can't even pretend to understand how you feel. You don't deserve this and I completely agree with you that you cannot continue as things are, whether you stay or go. I remember how your hard stance on cheating since secondary school. How you broke up with your boyfriend in school because he kissed one UDSS girl at a party. Those have always been your values. Just know this: whatever you decide, we are here for you. You will be fine. I will be praying for you"

NADIA: "Thank you Sis. It feels like a knife is churning through my insides and destroying everything in its wake. I know that I cannot stay in this condition. Not like this, my self respect will not permit me. My children deserve better.

Ken knows better. It's time for me to be true to my values. Oh, you remember Donald from FGC, lol. It feels so long ago, over a decade, I believe. I still think of my school mum advising me to continue the relationship, that it was just a kiss. But I knew better then. Lord, help me to stay true even at this time, may I find the courage to do the right thing, that's my sincere prayer.

Last Week

I moved out of the house with my two children. The last straw was our company lawyer. I saw them at a business cocktail making out. I asked the driver to take me home. He asked of my husband but I told him to leave him as he was busy. I got my kids and moved in with Preye temporarily till I found an apartment to stay.

Kenneth did not fight it. I think he was only concerned about the money and the children. I have made it clear that he could have access to them. I feel at peace because I had a plan. My Soul Sistas, true to their promise, have been with me through this. Sending me money, meals and love. All of them with their divergent opinions...

Mary, the Spirikoko, has called me everyday since to pray with me. She is convinced Kenneth will wake up one day and see the light. Who knows, he may. But I will not hang around waiting. However, the prayers and many forwarded scriptures has brought me peace and strengthened my faith.

Bukola, the Blamer, is still trying to find the person or people that lured Kenneth down this path. She is convinced it is not "ordinary". She kept sending me clues from her social media investigation of possibly guilty Lagos Girls. I had to ask her to stop. I could not be bothered whose charm worked on him. I wondered more why he was so fickle.

Njide, the Sharp Babe, made sure I got my finances in order. I only took about 30% of her advice but it landed me a sizable chunk to start another business and be comfortable with the kids. I wonder how her husband does not know of her portfolio of investments.

Aisha, I call her the Submissive, no let's make that **the Subservient** has been pleading with me. Bless her heart! She actually offered to go with me to beg Kenneth to take me back. I told her I respected her too much to put her through that. She is still trying to encourage me, saying she does not mind. I don't know how she does it... to diminish until only one person starts to matter in marriage is not how I planned my life.

The Shame Avoider, Iniobong, is carrying enough shame for both of us. She keeps scouring blogs and posts to see if someone has found out about our breakup. I secretly feel she pities me. She vehemently denies any rumor. I don't know how she thinks that helps but someday; she will come to face the inevitable. Who knows, she may not want to associate with a divorcee in future. Her reputation and associations are very important to her.

Preye, my Even-Keeled Reasoner, is so in touch with her core and is always advocating staying true to yourself, no matter the circumstance or the situation. Even though her logic is sound, sometimes it can be annoying because all you want sometimes is a soldier to cry on and a problem to mull over and linger on. Often, we know the truth but the courage to walk in it is lacking. Preye always lends you some of her courage to tide you over.

You would not believe **Ivie, the Egbe Wager!** The other day, we were at the Palms Shopping Mall when we saw Kenneth and the lawyer who I had nicknamed "The Final Straw". Ivie rushed to accost them and was almost fighting, shoving and cursing. I sat down and laughed while Kenneth pried her away. I think she got a few shoves in, don't ask me if it's right. I just know I enjoyed it.

Literally, I have Sistas who would go to war for me. Every woman, looking to draw a line in the sand and set healthy boundaries, needs friends and family like them.

THE CAR

Shameka was giddy with excitement and anticipation. She was literally floating around their 570 square feet apartment, moving from the only bedroom to the living room, stopping at the kitchen's island. She raised the cup in her hand and breathed the whiff of her ginger-peach herbal tea, eyes closed. This was her rejuvenation ritual.

Edosa was gone for weeks at a time at his job. He worked as a geologist in the industrial town of Odessa, South Texas, where the landscape teemed with oil rigs and dusty plains. He worked shifts: one week on, the other off in alternating schedules. Sometimes, he would get to cover for someone, and work three weeks straight. This was how he was making the money to pay back the high-interest student loans from his graduate school.

He was born in the United States but grew up in Nigeria. After his first degree at the University of Benin, he relocated to America. When he moved, he was only twenty-three, with little money in his pockets. He was grateful for a two-week stay at his distant cousins, before he set out to school. True, he had a partial scholarship to attend the University of Oklahoma, but to make up the difference he had taken out loans from the banks. As he had not been resident in the state for up to three years, he did not qualify for the more affordable government loans. He worked night shifts at the nursing home as an aide to make up money for his bills.

That was where Shameka met him. She was also a nurse's aide and had worked at Tender Care Nursing Home since she graduated high school three years ago. She lived on her own and was saving money diligently towards college. As a teenager, she knew that she wanted to be a Social Worker, helping children and those in need to solve problems and navigate life. She had the emotional mastery, the self-determination and empathy needed to do the job. Google and everyone warned that it did not pay much but she knew if she was financially prudent, she could make a good living.

Shameka had been on her own since 17. When her parents had decided to move to Alaska for a higher paying job, she opted to stay back. They were drowning in debt and kept chasing higher pay, to no avail. If they never reined in their spending and built a retirement plan, she doubted they would make headway.

But they had made their choices, she had a future to build for herself. She had already caught a vision that she was determined to walk in. Moreover, she had been adulting since she was old enough to work at 16 and had some money saved. She shared a flat with some cousins and kept working, all the while planning to pay her way through school. She would be the first in her family to graduate college, and she intended to work towards that possibility.

When she first met Edosa, she was taken in by his work ethic, his character and his intelligence. His Nigerian accent was definitely interesting, she had found it sexy. He spoke in that semi formal way she had come to find was cultural, calling folks Sir and Ma. The residents were all taken by him, he knew them by name, prefaced by Mr & Mrs, of course. He was easy and caring, always going the extra mile. But most of all, he was genuinely grateful for the opportunity to bring his dreams to fruition. That was why they took to each other: their shared visions of the future and all the hard work they were willing to put in to make them happen.

Three years later, he had graduated with a master's in Petrophysics Geology, while Shameka now had her associate degree in science from the community college. She had just enrolled for the bachelor's degree in Social Work. Through it all, she paid her way and continued working. Even though they were both making money now, they were a long way from paying off over $30,000 Edosa had obtained during his master's. That's why she wholeheartedly supported him working several weeks at a time. They were on track to pay off the bills in three years at the pace they were going. Seeing the capital reduce as they increased the payments excited Shameka.

They had gotten married after he graduated, with no plans for kids for the next couple of years. After all, they were young and had time. Debt was a dirty word to her, and she shared these principles of paying off debt, saving and investing with Edosa. Even though he was hard working, he did not necessarily seem to have a plan for his money when he started earning, till she stepped in. Seeing how her parents had carried student loans almost all their lives was not desirable for her. So, she planned her life with this ideal of frugality.

Edosa had told her he had a special surprise for her 25th birthday, which was today. It was a landmark birthday. He had made such a fuss and asked her to guess the gift. She had tried but after guessing a luxurious spa date, and even an outrageous latest iPhone, she had given up. But he kept promising that it will blow her mind so she could hardly contain her excitement.

"Honk, honk!!", The blaring horn from out front jolted her and her lips were scalded by the hot tea she was drinking. She had warned him to stop honking but Edosa said it was a Nigerian thing, and it was supposed to be endearing like "Honey, I'm home…". One of his many idiosyncrasies that she simply shook her head and laughed at now.

She walked out to the garage and found a strange sight. There was a car with a huge red bow on its hood. It was a brand-new Lexus sedan parked right next to her fifteen-year old Nissan Sentra. The car she named "Ryde o' Dye" with over 200,000 miles on it. At first, she thought he had won the car. "What is this, Edosa?" she said, eyes darting from car to his face and back again.

"A car, Shameka,"
"Whose is it. I don't understand..." her voice was trailing off.
"It is yours, My Love. Happy Birthday," he was grinning ear to ear.
"Boy, don't play with me. Stop fooling around please. Did you win it?" She was getting antsy now.

"No Baby, I got it for you. I want to say thank you for all you've been to me. I would never have made it in this America, if not for you. I love you with all my heart. Happy Birthday Shameka." His eyes were teary, and he walked over and held her hands, looking as proud as the day he walked across the stage to collect his diploma. "I've been wanting to do something like this since I met you. Thank God today, I finally have."

She smiled, thought and said, "I appreciate this gesture really I do. And I love you too." She kissed him warmly and rested her head on his generous chest. His heart was beating steadily as he cradled her one second longer. As they separated, he made to hand her the key. But she pushed it away, a firm look in her eyes.

He could sense the sassiness coming through. And he wondered out loud, “What’s the matter? Do you not like the color or would you prefer another model?”

She said, “I do like it... but unless you won the lottery, or someone gave you this as a gift. Please return this car to wherever you got it. We will not go into debt because of a car.”

He stood there, incredulous and feebly arguing. This was how his dad surprised him mum with a car. All his friends did this, the wives were always ecstatic and turned to social media to share their delight at the surprise and gratitude to their loving husbands. Shameka was supposed to be jumping for joy.

She sashayed back into the house, stopped in the doorway to say, “Hurry up, Boo... lunch is almost ready. The next time you get such a wild idea, be sure to check in with me first.”

He didn’t even get to answer before she shut the door in his face.

Three kids, no debt and one house later, they laugh about it all the time now but they never made any major financial commitments, without first talking about it. Edosa has stuck to perfume, flowers and spa gifts, since then.

GLOSSARY

Abeg
Please

Abeg I no wan hear anything wey go make me vex
"I don't want to listen to something upsetting"

Abi
Isn't it? (Yoruba)

Adire Boubou
Long maxi gown made of tire and dye fabric

Asoebi
Same fabric or uniform worn by many, usually for an event

Bendel
Former Nigerian state, now split into Edo and Delta State

Biko
Please (Igbo)

Dem dey wait us
"They are waiting for us"

Dem never born the person wey go try me
"The fellow that will contend with me is yet to be born"

Dem never born the woman wey wan carry me see road
"The woman to school me is yet to be born"

Dobale
Prostrate (Yoruba)

Egbe Wager
Hoodlum, troublemaker, stubborn, tough person (Urhobo)

Ehen?
Really? (Yoruba)

Ehn
A word/tone of enquiry

Ekaale
Good evening (Yoruba)

Gele
Tied and knotted head gear (Yoruba)

Ichie
A member of the King's traditional cabinet (Igbo)

I go beat shege commot from her head
I will beat the evil out of her (Hausa/pidgin)

Jare
An expression of exasperation

Kamkpogi, inu
"Let me call you/I will call you... okay/Do you hear me?"

Kayan mata
Herbal aphrodisiac. Literal: "Women's Property" (Hausa)

Ke
Intensifier (Yoruba)

Keke marwa
Auto-rickshaw (Lagos)

Kenneth dey craze
"Kenneth is Mad"

Madam no dey wait you?
"Is your madam not waiting for you?"

Mago-mago
Tricky

Mumu button
Point of weakness

Na
Is

Naim make-
That is the reason

Na my luck na
That is my luck. I gained.

Na she godey rush you
She will start seeking your attention

Na to do am strong tin
To harm or hurt someone

Ndinwanyi
Women folk (Igbo)

Nnoo o
Mother, used as a word of fondness for a female (Igbo)

Nwam
My child (Igbo)

O
Sound of emphasis. Used as an intensifier

Odogwu
Strong man (Igbo)

Oga
Boss (Yoruba)

Oko e nko
What about your husband? (Yoruba)

Oko mi
My husband

Okwaya?
"Isn't it?"

Omugwo
A period where a new mother and her baby are cared for.

Otiku niyen
"You are dead or "you are done for" (Yoruba)

Owigiri
Waist dance of the Ijaw tribe

Oya
Therefore. Come on (Yoruba)

Oyoyo
Beautiful young maiden (Igbo)

Pele
Apologies (Yoruba)

Se dada
I hope you are okay (Yoruba)

Sha
Regardless, used as an intensifier

Sharp-sharp
Quickly

She get belle?
"Is she pregnant?"

Suya
Beef or chicken Kebab (Hausa)

That one sef na husband?
"Is he a husband?" (Pejorative)

Waiyo
Expression of surprise (Hausa)

Waka-jugbe
Truant (Urhobo)

We sabi dem finish
They are completely known to us.

Wey dey enter eye
Attractive

Wey sabi road
The wiser ones or street smart

Who born dem
"How dare they?" or "They are not bold enough"

Your mumu don ripe o
"You are really fooli

APPENDIX

Your Action Plan on
HOW TO SET BOUNDARIES

HEY THERE, I want to let you in on a secret...

...it is a myth that love has no boundaries and that it is selfish to have them. So how can you set them? First, let me give you a premise.

You and your spouse, most likely, started your marriage as deep in love as possible, never intending to do each other harm and seeking to do right by each other.

However, we all have different perspectives in life, our values and culture and personalities inform those preferences of what we believe and how we want to be treated. It goes even further to determine how we treat others. That's why you may mean well but end up doing something that offends your partner and vice versa till you wonder how you can keep the peace and the love without compromising your values.

In ten steps, you will learn how to effectively set boundaries to give and receive love. Let me show you how...

Your BOUNDARIES BUDDY,

Bralade.

INTRODUCTION

How does it go wrong? Picture this: a gooey eyed couple taking their vows and committing to love each other for the rest of their lives yet few months or years later, it feels like Armageddon or like there is a huge distance between them in their home. What is it that causes these pure motives to either be misconstrued or to change completely? How do we go from love to endless conflict and distrust and in some cases, hate? Apart from dealing with truly evil people, the word is Boundaries.

> *"BOUNDARIES are property lines that signify ownership."*

BOUNDARIES vs. CONTROL

The ME vs YOU vs US triangle is best exemplified by an example Tony Evans, pastor and author of Kingdom Marriage, gives. He said at some weddings, the couple do the symbolic lighting of the unity candle where they each hold one lit candle to light a larger one in the middle. He explains that the mistake many make is to blow out their candle after lighting the third. Every person is born complete with their purpose, interests and values: to erase yourself in service to a marriage is not God's plan.

Key Premises are that our spouses have good intent and we cannot control others. In setting boundaries, you learn that the actions you take are based on what you have power over and who you have power over i.e. you. Influence with does not mean power over.

Note that boundaries are not about controlling other people but yourself. Boundaries are about being able to say no and receive a no in any relationship. True, these can have consequences that we will discuss shortly.

"BOUNDARIES are not about controlling someone else. You can only control YOU."

WHY BOUNDARIES?

"It is necessary and even vital, to set standards for your life and the people you allow in it". -Mandy Hale.

True love ultimately wants to treat the other person right. Think how much better it would be if they know, for certain, how you want to be treated. That is why communication is the bedrock of boundaries.

So how do we preserve ourselves and still commit to the aspiration of a unified home and marriage? We do it by setting boundaries. Here are the ten steps to defining and setting boundaries with your spouse and even other people.

Be sure to use the Action Plans that go with each step.

01. EDUCATE

First of all, you learn what your boundaries are based on your values and how you want to be treated. What are your non-negotiables? What are your red lines? What are the things you can control and what is out of your control? For example, you can let someone know that respect is an important value to you and you would prefer not to be yelled at.

Or infidelity and abuse are red lines for you that cannot be crossed. Obvious, you say? You would be surprised. Key thing to note is that no one is psychic and will not learn except there is intentional and vulnerable communication. This is a continuous feedback loop process, to learn and to teach as a couple as you grow together.

ACTION:
Don't assume: Educate your spouse on your Values and Boundaries.

02. IDENTIFY

Violations. What do violations to your boundaries look like? Are you keen to observe when your boundaries are crossed? The more we assume pure intent, the freer we are to identify and communicate where we have been hurt or what does not sit right with us.

Doing the inner work lets you know the situations and actions of our spouse that hurts and violates our boundaries. It also lets you know the issues out of your control.

ACTION:
Become aware. Review and identify things that hurt you

03. ACKNOWLEDGE

Your contribution to the problem. Many times, we are complicit in our own hurts because of lack of communication or enabling or harmful behavior. This is where two wrongs do not make a right. You can start the conversation by acknowledging and possibly apologizing for your part.

For example, "I apologize I never called you out for calling me names and yelling at me. Maybe you did not realize that it hurt". And then commit to communicating your boundaries or enforcing the appropriate consequences that we will discuss in the next few steps.

ACTION:
Be honest with yourself and acknowledge your part in it

04. REVIEW

Your action plan and consequences. After identifying what a violation to your boundaries is, you want to have an action plan for those circumstances. This will involve scenarios and your possible reactions in those cases.

Being proactive like this helps to prepare you and your partner for your reaction if these violations occur. Bear in mind, there are always new situations, so this review is also an ongoing activity.

For example, if he starts yelling at you or using insulting words, what do you want to do in that instance? You can plan to start by warning and then, if it persists, consider walking away from the situation.

Or the wife who keeps overspending and maxing out the credit card till your family finances are in jeopardy? Again, you may plan to have a conversation and also consider steps to limit access to the family's savings.

> *HAVE AN ACTION PLAN for when boundaries are violated*

05. CONFRONT

Your boundaries violator. Steps 1-4 are all largely introspective where you are taking stock, educating yourself on boundaries and preparing for communicating effectively in those instances when you confront your spouse.

For example, you can say, "Sweetie I don't know if you realize it, but you raised your voice at me." Key here is to maintain politeness and stick to the facts, no blame needs to be given here. Colossians 4:4 puts it well: "Let your speech always be gracious, seasoned with salt, so that you may know how you ought to answer each person."

ACTION PLAN Have those Crucial Conversations

06. SET CONSEQUENCES

Remember those consequences you decided on in REVIEW. During the confrontation, you set those consequences with your partner. Remember, the intent is not to control the other person, it is for your control.

So, instead of saying "you cannot do...", try saying "if you do... I will have to take such and such action", based on your action plan.

We change our behavior when the pain of staying the same becomes greater than the pain of changing.

"Consequences give us the pain that motivates us to change."
-Dr Henry Cloud

ACTION:
Decide on a consequence that is in your control

07. GIVE GRACE

People make mistakes. After all of these, assume good motives and intention. Remain calm when communicating and offer to explain further if your partner needs more clarity.

In addition, give your partner permission to speak their own mind to you. In leaving the door open, you can give as well as receive love and respect each other's boundaries.

When I speak with my husband on boundary issues, I do not raise my voice and I commit to speak politely. I am willing to engage in discussions, even where and when we disagree.

This is how I give grace. What about you?

ACTION:
Assume positive intent and give grace.

08. KEEP CONSEQUENCES

Act on your consequence. Don't be an enabler. "When we fail to set boundaries and hold people accountable, we feel used and mistreated," says Brené Brown, author of Daring Greatly. If you have previously communicated your plan of action, by all means keep it.

It is human nature to doubt your commitment if you do not honor your word. If you sit down and allow yourself to be called unprintable names or allow your career be derailed or go ahead with an activity you do not agree with, then consider that you are enabling the behavior.

ACTION PLAN Hold yourself and your spouse accountable

09. MAINTAIN YOUR BOUNDARIES

Having done all to stand. Have a good community of support around you. If may be that after you act on your consequence that your spouse retaliates or refuses to respect the boundary or withdraws from you.

This can be painful on both yourself and your spouse who may likely feel rejected. However, the consequence of doing nothing is just as painful. You may have "pseudo peace" but what it really means is that one person is bearing all the weight of the other person's actions.

Resentment from bearing hurt without speaking up serves no purpose when communication can help both your partner and you. Resist the temptation to rescue your spouse: "A man (or woman) of great wrath will pay the penalty, for if you deliver him, you will only have to do it again." (Proverbs 19:19)

ACTION PLAN Have the courage to engage instead of keeping it in and being bitter.

10. BEYOND BOUNDARIES

Maintain a good community. There are few associations as grounding and as secure as a tribe where you feel safe, heard and love.

A core group of people with whom you can be vulnerable and lean on for support. This same community that you willingly support as well when they need your help.

If you are going through a difficult time in your marriage, this is a life saver and even in smooth times, it still is a sure foundation that you can stand on.

Nurture these relationships and do not violate their trust as they keep yours. Pray for each other and provide a safe place.

ACTION:
Be intentional about your tribe

CONCLUSION

If you take these steps, you will be acting as a good steward of the greatest treasure that has been committed to you i.e. yourself.

That is why to keep effective boundaries with others, you must first keep boundaries with yourself and respect the boundaries of other people. Staying true to your values is not selfish, it is how you fully contribute to any relationship you commit to. Keep growing and evolving in your values. Keep boundaries with yourself.

Signs of Healthy Boundaries include:

- being able to say no without guilt
- staying true to your values
- being free to pursue your own goals & passions
- taking responsibility for your happiness
- not having to rescue others from the consequences of their own behavior
- feeling safe enough to disagree and saying yes not because of the pressure of pleasing others.

Essentially, having Healthy Boundaries is the highest level of self-awareness: knowing who you are, what you believe, what your limits are and having the courage to communicate that.

YOU ARE WORTHY OF LOVE

"Let no one disregard you" (Titus 2:15). Not even you should disregard you.

"The extent to which two people in a relationship can bring up and resolve issues is a critical marker of the soundness of a relationship" says Henry Cloud, a Christian psychologist and Boundaries Expert. Boundaries are the keys to giving and receiving love. It takes courage to engage and be vulnerable. "I'm never more courageous than when I'm embracing imperfection, embracing vulnerabilities, and setting boundaries with the people in my life."

You are a truly special person, worthy of love and belonging, free to achieve your goals and fulfil your purpose, "Let no one disregard you" (Titus 2:15), including yourself. Keep speaking your truth in love and living within your boundaries.

Have a happier life and marriage as you set those boundaries today!

ACKNOWLEDGEMENTS

"If you want to fast, go alone. If you want to go far, go together".

I have been privileged to have so many with me on this journey. This first-time author's heart is filled with so much gratitude for the many who have inspired, encouraged and worked hard to make this book a reality.

"Behold, I stand at the door and knock. If anyone hears my voice and opens the door, I will come in to him and eat with him, and he with me." (Rev 3:20) Thank you God Almighty for being the Ultimate Example in Boundaries. And you gave me an answer for everyone who asks if setting limits are biblical. My faith in you is my anchor and the reason for boundaries.

My husband of a decade, Obioha Tobechukwu Anthony Emenanjo, you inspired this book with the love and respect you show me daily. Thank you for asking me diligently and ceaselessly about the progress of this book. Sometimes that was the reason I wrote, to give you an update. Thank you for believing and buying into dreams you never saw and all the pie in the sky ideas I keep sharing. You have a heart without guile and a love that is laced with logic and limits. I love you more than words can say.

My children, Faith's Child Chude Perezi, Genius Eloka Tantua and Rambunctious Karena Adaoha, thank you for putting up with a Mummy who went everywhere with a pen and journal for months on end, whose bursts of inspiration meant play could not continue, sometimes. You are the reason for everything.

It is unfair to have the kind of family I have, they set me up for success and a life of significance. A family of love, logic, respect and healthy limits. Seiyifa and Grace Koroye, my parents to whom I owe my love for literature and my perspectives on love and life. Your example continues to give and teach. You never quite taught with words but simply by being.

My one and only sister, Adi, whose first feedback of this book to me were typos neither myself or the editor never saw, thank you for your keen eye and your generosity. Ever ready to support. Your husband, Eze is blessed. My brothers, their spouses (now my siblings) and their children ground me daily:

Funkeme & Vivian, Tonbra & Ekaro, Ayibanua and Cindy, God bless you for sustaining the love we share. My nieces and nephews give me hope that the legacy will endure.

To be surrounded by strong and salient women is to become one: to my Aunties, Professor Engobo Emeseh, you are my role model and mentor, in spirit and in truth. You first told me "Start As You Mean To Go On" and I have never stopped. Dr. Mrs. Stella Ugolo, who you are is an indefatigable leader and relentless lover. Thank you for always being proud of me, sometimes for no reason.

My grandad, Atangbala, Tangodi Koroye: for all the newspapers and books you made me read out loud from when I was five years old. Your eyes may have been blind, but your ears were ever so sharp and your brain was a phenomenon. You made me love words in every art form. Okoide, Sir. Your legacy lives. My cousins, aunties and uncles of the Koroye and Aguamah family. Adoh. I know you will carry me as an Olotu. My mother in law, Lady Florence Emenanjo aka Nne, your quiet strength and faithful devotion is inspiring. Thank you for receiving me. I may be the only one in the universe blessed to have seven sisters in love: Adaobi, Chinye, Nkeihuka, Nweize, Ijeoma, Judith and Ndubuisi and your spouses, especially Chike, my fellow Go-Getter. Thank you for loving your "Blackie" and quirky sis just as she is and supporting my every endeavour.

My cousin Yinke: your casual assumption of my boundless abilities is both annoying and inspiring. The support you give me allows me focus. Thank you for reading every story and spreading the word.

To have friends like mine is to have sisters for life. This sisterhood bears me up and sustains me with prayers, prophecies and presents. Oyintonbra, Ijeoma, Chrissie, Alaere and Ebiere, it all started with the visions we cast. Now, see us running with them. Tonbra, my Twinnie, we have walked hand in hand, across seas and through trials. Thanks for having my back. Ijay, your perception is second to none. Thank you for the voicenote motivation boosts whenever the going got tough and the pace slowed.

Pastor Bukola Usidame, how are you like this? You learned how to plan a book launch because of “A Line in The Sand”. Thank you for rallying the troops and spearheading publicity. Nkechi Amadi, girl you make me feel like a star! Ebiere Bolu, wholehearted and wise you are. Thank you.

Uzoamaka, Eileen, Ekene, Nkechi, Doite and Adaeze, thank you for adopting this project as your own. Uloma & Nina, you show up for me constantly.

I have friend-mentors: MULA, I see you. Ehi, you are the Hype. Eden, the Sage: you drip wisdom and love. My Houston

Babes: Ngowari, Uloma, Nina, Angela, Ijeoma, Ibiere, Pamela and Margaret. Thank you. Ikechukwu and Uduak, I appreciate your faith in me.

My beta readers. I reached out to my fellow voracious readers from childhood and they delivered serious criticism, but they never made me feel less: thank you Joy and Oladebi for not holding back.

This book has been handled by editors, proof-readers and publishers. Ijeawele, I would say you are Chimamanda reincarnated if she were not still alive. You say I believe in you, I think it is the other way round. You were the eyes waiting to see every story and edit every word. Once you said "Big Sis, this story is like egusi soup that is inconsistent: watery and half-done". I am still angry. Lol. The world will see your brilliance.

Ebi Akpeti Woodson, I remember reading "God Has a Sense of Humor". I never dreamed I could but you showed the way. You were supposed to be just a beta reader, but you turned editor. Thank you for your counsel. Michael Afenfia, for taking the time to read and validating this concept.

Gabriel David, thank you for working to make this book a reality. Asari Otu, God saved the best for last with you. Thank you for proofreading and then continuing to bug me to turn it all in. If you ever need me, just call. Stephen Angbulu, Nnamdi Obi, thank you for the work you put in. The team: Waidou, John and Lammy, God bless you. Fola Folagbade of Worital, my publisher, ever so courteous and meticulous, thank you for bringing this book to life. Any mistakes you see are not theirs, they are all mine because my particular self may not have accepted all their corrections.

I have a coach and a mentor. Fela Durotoye, Egbon Mi, is the latter. Thank you for being a true big brother and for the words you spoke concerning this book. For the Speak For Gold community. My coach of life, friend & sister, Debola Deji-Kurunmi, the wisdom that has been granted you is stupefying. Thank you for your message on multi-potentiality and how to hone strengths. For your teachings on personal power and purpose.

Ekene Onu, the iconic womanhood coach, thank you for the brand of women you are raising, with healthy boundaries. You are inspiring. Paul Foh, you show up daily and you push. Thank you so much. Minda Harts, thank you for your writing retreat; it set me on course. Dr Nicolya Williams: your writing course was a great resource. Laju Iren, you truly were born for this. Samuel Iwar, thank you for your example of a secure Nigerian man with boundaries. Evelyn, thank you for giving me a chance. I hope I make you proud.

The communities I belong to provided me nourishment and nurture through the arduous task of writing and publishing. Speak for Gold family, Immerse Inner Circle, Iconic Womanhood, Firebrand, KGWA, Society of Women Engineers, Becoming, my Dow family. My ALITS Mastermind, you put up your hands to help with this book and you have delivered, over and over again. You know yourselves; you will never lack people.

To pastors, ministers and clergy who keep perfecting me in the faith, thank you. Henry Cloud and John Townsend, thank you for your research, study and books on Boundaries. The work you do matters; it liberates and empowers. It is my honor to perpetuate your message.

All my stories were fiction, but I got a good dose of inspiration from the seed these people and many others planted: Stella Uzochukwu for A Different Set of Rules, The Ighalos for The Car, Chude, My StarBoy, for A Line In The Sand.

If it sounds like your story, don't worry I did not spy on you but maybe the universe is asking you to draw a line in the sand and close that chapter so you can love freely, be loved and fulfil purpose. Thank you for your courage, Reader. It is your picture I have carried in mind from the beginning. Come through for you. Set healthy boundaries. Live your best life.

To all who have gifted this book and have held book clubs, thank you for owning this message. You make the difference. "The Lord gave the word: great was the company of those that published it." (Psalm 68:11). I could not possibly have written every name, but you know yourself and the word of advice or encouragement you gave. Thank you so much.

SHARE YOUR EXPERIENCE

I know you have had quite the experience reading this book.

REVIEW

Please leave a review on Amazon, Goodreads and other book sites.
On social media, use the hashtag #ALITS and #ALineInTheSandBook.
I will be reading every one of them. Can't wait to hear from you!

BOOKCLUB

Download your bookclub resources on my website: www.bralade.com
And have a fun and memorable discussion with your group.

LIBRARY

Request this book at your local library.
Or write to me to get one for your library.

AUTHOR CONTACT

Send an email or connect. Would love to chat with you.

Website:
www.bralade.com

Email: hello@bralade.com

Social Media:
@Bralade Koroye-Emenanjo on LinkedIn, Facebook, Twitter.
@iambralade on Instagram.
@Bralade on YouTube.
#ALineInTheSandBook #ALITS
#TheBoundariesMovement

MORE BOOKS BY THE AUTHOR

COMING SOON!
The Book of Kiles: Pride & Wisdom in a Title
Co-authored by Bralade Koroye-Emenanjo & Seiyifa Koroye.

This work is a curation of the rich cultural heritage of titles and praise names (kiles) that herald men and women of stature in their tribes. The authors expound on the pride and wisdom in these poetic phrases by bringing a modern context into this practice. The rituals surrounding their delivery and the sagacity are the gift of the Ijaw tribe to the world. Over one hundred of these kiles are contained in this coffee-table book, paired with beautiful, indigenous photos and artwork.

The second book in the PWYP Book Series will be available, late 2021.

Made in the USA
Columbia, SC
01 February 2025

53101503R00148